B.L. OVERMAN

THE
YONI FLOWER

THE PRIMEVAL ONES UNIVERSE
(IN CHRONOLOGICAL ORDER)

Primeval Ones: Parasites of Pleasure Series:

The Amazonian Uteroboscis (Book 1)
Uteroboscis: **Outbreak** (Book 2)

Primeval Ones: Plants of Pleasure Series:

The Yoni Flower (Book 1)
Lizzy's Flower Glizzy (A Tie-in Novella) (Book 1.5)
Blight of The Yoni Flower (Book 2) *(The Uteroboscis & Yoni Flower* Crossover **1***)*
Flesh Forest (A Tie-in Novella) (Book 2.5)

Primeval Ones: Deities of Lust Series:
The Horned One (Book 1) (The Uteroboscis & Yoni Flower Crossover **2***)*
The Flowered Goddess (Book 2)

And there will be more pleasure organisms & gods of lust to *come!*

B.L. OVERMAN

THE
YONI FLOWER

SCIROTIC
BOOKS
Scirotic.com

***SCIROTIC
BOOKS***
An Imprint of Masterless Press

Scirotic.com

The Yoni Flower
Copyright © 2022 by B.L. Overman
Cover design by Thea Magerand

First Scirotic Books print edition: February 2022

Printed in the United States of America

ISBN: 979-8-9856127-0-7 (print)
ISBN: 979-8-9856127-1-4 (ebook)

FOREWORD & *CONTENT WARNING*

If you're a reader from Literotica, or if you're coming here from *The Amazonian Uteroboscis*, hello again! If you're new, welcome, dear reader, to the Primeval Ones Universe—a universe where phallic organisms who evolved to deliver pleasure and lustful beings who want nothing more than to mate are slowly beginning to be discovered in uncharted regions of our current world by adventurers and scientists alike. *The Yoni Flower* is the second book in the Primeval Ones series, so if you like erotic and weirdly fascinating tales with epically bizarre and naughty crossovers, **sign up** at **Scirotic.com** for updates & ***FREE*** reads from **The Primeval Ones Universe**! If you like your erotica to have more than just vividly described, naughty passages, you're in luck! An immersive, living world with a mystery to unravel lies ahead along with some scientifically sound research to make it feel that much more realistic. Also, Allie Hannigan, the intelligent heroine of this novel, is a botanist who works throughout the story with the other science-loving ladies in her life to study and understand her discovery.

The Yoni Flower [as well as the other books to *come*] is an erotic horror/sci-fi, splatterpunk story intended for adults who are into tentacle stuff, monster erotica, and Lovecraftian tales of titillation. As such, the text ahead will contain *very* graphic descriptions of Allie doing naughty things with a phallic flower that oozes sap and splooges all sorts of hot cream. Fair warning, gross things happen to her after the gooey fun is over (***cough, cough*** Chapter 4). And some pretty messed up stuff happens to her friends later on. Oh, and there's a pretty gross scene with her one-night-stand too… So, if you're not into splatterpunk, there are quite a few chapters ahead that may be disturbing for those who are uncomfortable with imagery intended to elicit a certain gross-out factor. Because of that, *The Yoni Flower* may not be suitable for all readers. Girl-on-plant fun aside, there will also be explicit details of freaky sex scenes with F/M & F/F partners as well as solo play, and strong language.

All characters are over 18 years of age and any sexual acts described in the pages ahead are for entertainment purposes and not as a resource for sex-ed.

Enjoy the read! And prepare to be left feeling entertained and uncomfortable in the best way!

CHAPTER 1
ECOSEXUAL

Saturday, May 28

There are roughly 611 miles of trail to explore in Olympic National Park, but here I am all alone and way off the official path, purposefully wandering deeper and deeper into this mossy wonderland. Not smart considering a thousand people have purportedly vanished without a trace here since 1916, but I wouldn't be doing this if my dad hadn't raised me from the age of seven to be an expert-level hiker and wilderness survivalist. And it's not like this is my first time doing this. In the three years since turning 18, I've spent a few days per month purposefully losing myself in the wilderness. Because I love feeling like I'm discovering untouched pockets of nature where there are no other people—because I don't particularly like most people, and I love being surrounded by plants.

The other reason I also really love hiking a lot? Because I eat like crazy and this is how I stay slim and fit.

To keep from getting lost forever, I try to follow one bearing on my compass each time I wander off-trail. For this adventure, that direction is northeast from where I deviated off of the Hoh River Trail. During my trailless adventure, I frequently use my cellphone to snap pictures of landmarks, then I update my topographical map with their approximate locations accordingly.

On top of that, I also mark trees with this biodegradable, neon orange tape near said landmarks, just in case I lose the map or my three portable solar charges die on me. As an additional means of maintaining my bearings, I've also been hiking along this small stream I found about a mile off-trail, following it uphill through soft, dense ferns and clusters of moss-covered trees. Based upon the speed of the stream's current, it's safe to assume it's leading me to a much larger body of water that I'm hoping is a hidden lake with crystal clear waters or a gorgeous waterfall—somewhere I can skinny dip and take a nice cool bath.

About two miles into the off-trail exploration, I discover a small, muddy clearing right where the stream has widened into a creek with slightly more turbulent waters. Perpendicular to it, there's a gigantic, fallen log that's overgrown with moss.

Oh, I want to lay across that so bad, I think, hurrying over to it.

The width of the horizontal lying trunk is, like, waist-high to me, so it takes a bit of effort to climb up on it. As I kneel against the damp, fuzzy carpet of moss, I hike up my skirt then straddle it like a horse.

After removing my backpack and dropping it onto the ground, I lean forward and lay belly down on the fallen tree, resting my cheek against the soft layer of spongy leaves as my arms wrap around the log. I don't know if it's because of how my panty-covered vagina just grinded against the moss just now or if it's because of all these delicious earthy, floral smells in the air, but I just got super horny and damp out of nowhere…

While I lay here, all I can think about is sitting back up, pulling my panties aside, and grinding my bare pussy against this moss-covered wood, riding it like it's a mechanical bull until I'm on the edge of climax. That's when I'd lay on my back and finger-blast myself to completion.

As I'm sitting up to carry out my botanical fantasy, I spot this straight, branchless stick near the edge of the creek that is completely covered in moss.

Oh my gawd, I think, climbing off of the log and skipping over to it. Upon picking up the twig that's as wide around as my pinky and about five inches long, I use two fingers to stroke it from mossy tip to mossy tip. There isn't even a spec of wood visible through the green fuzz, and it's smooth all the way down—not one sharp growth or bump sticking out of it. *It's perfect!*

With my nature-provided sex toy in hand, I skip back to the log and straddle it just like before. Once I find a patch where the moss is thickest and the bark underneath is smoothest, I scoot up to it, pull my panties aside, and then I grind against it nice and slow, humping it the way I used to do with my pillow years ago. Having wet, fuzzy moss rubbing against my clit and brushing against my folds feels amazing, but it's not enough. I need penetration, like, now.

After bucking against it for another minute or so, a climax starts to build, so I lay back and spread my labia apart before teasing my entrance with the smoothest end of the twig. "Ah," I moan as I slowly impale my slick passage with the mossy stick.

Humping fallen moss-covered logs, diddling myself with sticks and stems—this is the other reason I like to wander off in the middle of nowhere all by myself like this. I'm what some would call an Ecosexual, meaning I have a kink for pleasuring myself with anything of the earth, especially when it's the color of my eyes— green irises speckled with brown. Name a vegetable or fruit that's long and somewhat tubular and I've probably masturbated with it. Carrots, bananas, Asian eggplant, and cucumbers are my usual go-to natural toys of choice. Their existence is the reason I don't own a dildo. And for those fruits and veggies that aren't shaped like dicks—such as apples, watermelons, and mangoes—I slice them up and either toy myself with them or I just slide them inside of me and birth them out over and over.

I've stuffed my hole with fresh leaves, flowers, roots, edible mushrooms, grapes, and even chestnuts that were still in their spikey husks.

One time, after purchasing veggies at an Asian market, I went into the bathroom then I shoved the dirty white bulb end of Bok Choy into my vagina. I spent all day walking around with it stuffed in me until I got home. That's when I masturbated with it before sautéing it up for dinner.

I've masturbated with vines and even branches not covered in smooth moss.

I've fucked myself with the soil-caked bulb at the bottom of a tulip that I dug up from my garden, using that flower like it was a skinny dildo.

Sometimes I even like to pack my vagina with soil then finger myself until I'm gushing a muddy mess. That is, unless I find a nice patch of mud that smells deliciously earthy, then I just fill myself with muck and masturbate with my fingers or whatever is around.

This probably goes without saying, but sticking soil and unclean vegetation inside my vadge has obviously led to me popping antibiotics like vitamins a few times per year. It's because my bizarre kink comes with the risk of frequent vaginal infections that I ended up befriending my OB/GYN, Dr. Sloane Quinn. And to keep from seeing her more than I need to, I've followed her instructions and started taking probiotic vaginal suppositories as a means of prophylaxis to lower my odds of infection. Thankfully, I did just that before leaving my tent this morning.

"Ugh-ah," I groan when my climax nears critical mass.

Now I start rubbing my clit more vigorously while toying myself with a bit more speed, wincing from the friction of the twig's now more noticeable roughness.

"AHH!" I scream as my toes curl and my vagina contracts around the stick. My body trembles so hard from the sweet release that I almost roll off the log.

It takes a few minutes after my orgasm before I can get myself to sit up. After fingering the bits of moss out of my pussy, I whip back my auburn curls, hop off the log, sling my pack over my shoulder, then continue along the creek.

About twenty minutes or so later, I start catching a whiff of something sweet that seems to get stronger every few feet. *Why does it feel like I'm getting a buzz?*

Five minutes later, I emerge from the dense brush and spot this mini waterfall where water is rushing down lush, green-carpeted rocks into a crystal-clear pond. It's not until I approach the waterfall that I realize that the same wonderfully sweet scent I've been catching whiffs of for the last quarter mile is even stronger here, hanging over the area like an invisible cloud of the most delicious perfume.

"Mmmm," I moan, taking a nice deep breath of the heavenly aroma. Almost immediately, I'm overcome with this elation and excitement that makes my nipples hard and makes my dampening vaginal walls twitch.

Holy shit, why am I so horny? It's like I didn't just masturbate half-an-hour ago…

Sniffing rapidly like a bloodhound, I try tracking down the source of this fragrance, following the scent to where it's the strongest. My nose leads me around the waterfall to a path of mushy soil between the rocks and the wall of trees. A few yards later, the sweet, earthy scent grows more intense. And the closer I get to it, the dizzier and more aroused I become.

Geez, Allie Hannigan, why the heck are you so horny right now? I inhale deeply through my nose in rapid puffs, relishing in the smell of sugar, vanilla, and honey. *This smell… Whatever it is has me feeling so fucking good! It's got to be a pheromone-like aphrodisiac of some kind. But from what? I'm a botanist, and I can't think of any plant in the Olympic National Forest that smells like this or induces arousal in mammals. There's nothing like that anywhere in the Pacific Northwest for that matter…*

Through the brush ahead, there's a tight circle of moss-clad, bigleaf maple trees encompassing this grassless, shaded clearing. In the dead center of the clearing, there's one ginormous, leafless Sitka spruce. The dead spruce not only towers above all the rest, but it's also the widest—maybe 15 feet across. And, in the middle of its massive trunk, there is a 10 to 12-foot wide and maybe 8-foot-high hollow that tunnels right through it.

No way…

As beautiful as the sight is, that's not what has me captivated. It's the thing growing up from the dark soil in the middle of that spacious hollow that makes my pussy instantly dampen and throb with urgent need.

CHAPTER 2
THE PHALLUS IN THE HOLLOW

Saturday

Rising out of a maybe six-inch-high dirt mound that's longer than it is wide, there's a lone, *very* phallic-looking plant that lacks chlorophyll or colorful pigment of any kind. And by phallic, I mean that the thing growing from the thick white stalk that's jutting out of the soil mound is a fleshy, beige spadix that looks like a cock. The thing even has a bulbous tip that resembles the glans of a human penis almost to a T...

With my heart racing in excitement, I hurry through the brush and move hastily across the circular clearing toward the unusual and beautiful plant growing in the tree's hollow. The closer I get to it, the more potent the sweet, floral odor becomes. The air is so thick with the fragrance, I can taste it, like I've walked into a dense fog of invisible nectar. Each time I inhale, I become dizzier and more delirious with arousal.

I've never smelled anything this delicious in my life! Seriously, my mouth is drooling, and so is my pussy.

Upon reaching the entrance to the Sitka spruce's hollow, I set my backpack down right in the threshold before approaching the ghastly flower. Now that I'm right in front of it, I realize this plant resembles a more penis-like version of the Amorphophallus bulbifer—or Voodoo Lily—plant, but instead of having an upward-facing spathe leaf that surrounds the spadix like a cup, the five thick flower petals dangling from the base of the phallus's shaft have their arrowhead tips pointing toward the earth. The way the meaty petals are draped down around the thick stalk makes it look like it has starfish arms that are trying to hug a pole.

I grin when it occurs to me what this thing resembles. "This plant looks like a dick wearing a skirt made of giant banana peels." I giggle as I kneel before the specimen. Now I begin snapping some pictures on my iPhone. "What should I name you?" Since it looks like a plant from the arum genus with an inverted spathe, decide I'll call it a skirted arum. Or maybe I'll call it Priapos Euphallus—a true phallus. That, as opposed to the Amorphophallus, or the misshapen phallus.

There is nothing misshapen about this beautiful flower's spadix. It looks more like a dick than the last dick I saw.

The phallus is maybe 3 to 4 inches in diameter, similar to the stalk below, and 8 or 9-inches long from the glans-like head to where the beige petals begin to split like a banana peel. Basically, it has the dimensions of an actual cock. Even the way the peach-colored veins on the pale, cream-colored skin of the spadix make it look like a penis.

With two fingers, I caress the strange plant from the leathery, waxy petal skirt up the smooth shaft to the bulbous tip. *Um, why is this thing warm to the touch? It's in the shade…*

While I caress it, my other hand wanders up my skirt so I can give my needy clit a rub over my drenched panties. The shaft feels so much like skin that, if my eyes were closed, I wouldn't know it wasn't a man's member. Touching it like this sets me into an even worse fit of arousal. Unless that's just this intoxicating fragrance doing this to me…

Upon curling my fingers around the spadix and giving it a gentle squeeze, I'm shocked to find that it's surprisingly firm yet a bit squishy, just like actual an erect cock…

"Oh my fuck…" I whisper, lightly stroking it from the middle of the shaft to the tip.

As my curled thumb and forefinger bump into the base of the spadix's bulbous glans, the shaft throbs ever so subtly between my grip. Then, from the quarter-inch-wide hole at the center of the cockhead, a clear, yellowish secretion oozes out of it, beading up like precum until the liquid glob gets so big that gravity sends it dripping down onto my finger.

"Is this nectar?" I whisper to no one but myself as I release the spadix and sniff the secretion.

God, it smells like the sweetest, most delicious of fruits…

With the finger that was rubbing my clit, I wipe up the secretion and rub it against the pad of my thumb. The liquid is pretty thick and incredibly slippery, much like raw egg whites. And when I pull my finger away from my thumb, a glistening strand of goo stretches between my digits like a heavy rope of snot. As tempted as I am to suck my fingers clean, I'm unsure if this sap is poisonous or not. So, instead of slurping it all up, I simply touch the tip of my tongue to the plant ooze to see if I have an adverse reaction.

"MMM!" I moan, smacking my lips.

The sap, or whatever it is, tastes like a mix between maple syrup and candied cherries!

Despite my previous reservations, I can't help but lick up the rest of the glistening goodness.

As I swish the deliciousness around in my mouth, I stroke the warm spadix until it oozes twice as much sap as before. Right before it dribbles down the shaft, I wipe up the secretion with my middle finger, reach back up my skirt, pull aside my panties, then lube up my slit with the sliminess.

I need to know if it will irritate my vagina, I think, plunging the sap-covered digit into my tight, slick cavity. *Because I desperately want to fuck this plant... No... I have to fuck this plant. I have to...*

While I pleasure myself, my free hand caresses its way down the plant's shaft to the skirt of smooth petals. My gentle touch makes the spadix pulsate slowly again, causing it to spurt out stream after stream of syrupy sap that slowly trickles down its length. The more I tease it, the more viscousness it excretes. Eventually, the entire shaft is glistening with a yellow sheen like it's lubing itself up for me.

The urge to lick the sweetness off of the flower is impossible to resist, so I end up dragging my tongue from the base of the spadix's shaft to the cockhead, and then I mindlessly engulf the whole bulbous head with my mouth like it's a lollipop, slurping up a tongue-full of the secretion straight from the hole like it's a straw.

"MMMM!" I moan, gulping down the deliciousness before pulling the spadix from my mouth with a loud smack.

Now I watch in awe as it throbs and spurts more sap than ever before, my mouth flooding with saliva the entire time. *No more,* I think, clenching my teeth and clamping my glazed lips shut. *I need to save some of this heavenly lube for when I ride it...*

Resisting the urge to consume anymore this thing's godly sap, I lean back then I lift one of the five waxy petals that are the size of my hand. The thick thing is surprisingly heavy and dense, like a slab of meat.

It's not colorless after all, I think when I see the glistening, slightly wrinkly underside of the petal. It's not a beige like the outside, but a vibrant reddish-pink that reminds me of watermelon, and it's webbed with deep-red veins. Texture-wise, it looks just like the fleshy petals of a Stapelia schinzii succulent if it was lined with the rugae-like flesh of a moist vagina.

"Oh my…" I gasp as my middle two fingers glide across the underside of the petal up toward the crease between the petal and the stalk. It's surprisingly warm, which is odd for a plant. Also, it somehow feels just as soft and smooth as my vaginal walls do against the finger currently pumping in and out of me. Just as soft, but two times as slick, like I'm fingering a slimy aloe vera. "This is the most amazing fucking thing I've ever touched…" I moan breathily. It's so wet and tight that, when I begin fingering the tight crease between the petal and stalk with quick pumps, it gushes louder than my pussy is right now even though I'm super wet and vigorously masturbating. "This plant—" I whimper as I curl my fingers against my G-spot.

This plant's top half is like a cock and the underside of it is like a pussy… How? Why did it evolve like this? What is this thing?

When I pull my fingers out from underneath the thick petals, they're slick with a clear, colorless coating. While it is slippery, it's a bit sticky, and it's nowhere near as viscous as what oozed out of the tip. Honestly, it's more like vaginal secretions than anything. And, speaking of vaginal secretions, there's all sorts of sticky squelching going on between my legs as my vigorous finger-fucking sends more juices than I've ever produced before dripping down my digits.

Are these plant secretions making me wetter? I moan so loudly that the birds in the trees above caw and fly off. Arousal quickly builds like a ready-to-explode pressure cooker. *God… I feel… anxious… like… fingers aren't enough to give me the sweet release I crave. My pussy is aching with a need I've never felt before, like I might die if I don't get something long and wide in me now…* Panting, I stare longingly at the golden-glazed shaft before me. *It's been a few minutes since I licked up that sap and started fingering myself with it, so it's probably safe to fuck myself with this strange plant without having to worry about any adverse reactions.*

After setting up my camera to record what's about to go down, I yank down my panties and kick them off to the side. With my dress hiked up, I squat over the skirted dick-like plant. Just like I would with a guy I'm about to ride, I hold the spadix in place with my thumb and pointer then lower myself onto it until the slick, bulbous knob of its tip parts the dangling meat curtains of my inner labia.

"Oof," I sigh out when the girthy tip glides in and bulges through my tight opening. It's such a delicious feeling, I savor the experience by impaling my cavity with the thing as slowly as possible. "Auuugh-ohh!" is the throaty sound I make as the phallus's slick head drags against my G-spot, my cry of pleasure echoing inside the tree's hollow.

That's when I release the spadix and reach underneath the petals so I can hold the flower by the stalk. The erect stem is rubbery to the touch and it feels firm like a muscular snake when I squeeze it. Like the spadix, it throbs ever so slowly in my grip.

Inch by inch, the naturally lubed phallus slips deeper into me, filling me the way I've needed since I first smelled it. When it bumps into my cervix, I rise off of it until the cockhead is about to pop out of me, then I squat back onto it a bit faster. My core spasms as my pussy swallows it as deep as it'll go. The length of it, its girth, the warmth of its *skin*, the way its fleshy phallus feels gliding against my tight flesh—it's almost indistinguishable from a well-endowed man's cock. Actually, it feels so much better than a dick, because it's constantly throbbing gently inside of me while also coating itself with this incredibly slippery sap that I swear is making my pussy tingle with pleasure and making everything feel more intense. There's also this weird stretching sensation deep in my vagina that sort of feels like I'm dilating or something… I don't hate it, but I don't love it either…

A few bounces later, my legs go weak from pleasure and I almost fall, catching myself by planting my hand in the soil below. The stalk bends with me, but it doesn't snap, thankfully. Since it seems sturdy and flexible, I unwrap my hand from around it and I begin bouncing on it a bit faster—a bit rougher, basically hate-fucking it. In response, the plant's throbbing grows more rapid, and I swear it feels like it's swelling inside of me.

No, it is definitely swelling inside me, I think after the pleasure makes my vagina repeatedly clench around it. *It feels like it's stretching me out in the best way.*

With each descent, I take it as deep as my sex will allow, letting it batter my cervix. The longer I go at it, the harder and faster I ride it. Every time I writhe and grind down onto it, my pussy gushes louder and louder. During each ascent from its *base*, my sap-filled cavity squelches like a boot being pulled out of thick mud. And when I look down to adjust my footing, I stare in awe at the slowly expanding puddle of clear, yellowish syrup pooled around the stalk beneath me.

At one point, right as I'm about to orgasm—right as the head of the spadix is bulging in my tight entrance, my pussy clenches like a vice, squeezing the slippery cock-plant so hard that it launches out of me with a sticky-sounding bloop. When I look down at the slimy, throbbing phallus, I find that it is *definitely* girthier than it was when I first saw it. Not only is it girthier, but when I hold it place for reinsertion, the skin of it feels mushy and tacky to the touch, like a peeled banana that's been sucked on vigorously or masturbated with—a messy texture I know all too well from doing both things to bananas.

It's not dissolving, is it? I drag a finger across the pulpy slime coating it, stopping when my gaze falls onto these four thin, semitransparent white vines sticking out of the sap-spurting hole. *Also, what are these little things?*

I don't care why vines are growing out of the tip of the spadix or that the phallus is swelling, I just slide the bulbous, knob of head back and forth between my slit until the engorged thing pops back inside of me, then I drop down on it until it fills me to end of my canal.

To better help me bounce on the cock-plant without falling over, I lean back a bit then plant my hands in the soft soil right behind my ass the way I do to a guy's thighs when I ride him cowgirl. Now that I'm basically perched in a crab walk pose, I look up at the hollow's bark ceiling while I fuck the plant's phallic rod even harder and faster than before.

It only takes six seconds for my climax to build back to the brink of ecstasy. Right when I'm on the edge, I maneuver back into a squat and use a dirt-covered hand to rub my sap-glazed clit.

It only takes two more bounces on the spadix before sweet release strikes like a heavenly lightning bolt from within. For a split second, my vision goes white as the mother of all orgasms explodes below, sending waves of pleasure and bliss surging through every fiber of my being.

The intensity of my climax makes my legs go so weak that I wind up dropping down onto the spadix harder than intended, slamming my cervix against the bulbous head right as my vaginal walls clench around the swollen shaft. My body quakes so hard that I lose my balance and topple over backward, the rigid stalk bending with me all the way down while my cramping love muscle keeps the still ballooning spadix from slipping out. A second after my ass hits the dirt, the phallus throbs hard once, twice. On the third throb—the hardest throb—this powerful jet of warm sludge blasts right up against my cervix, and damn does it feel fantastic.

Holy shit! There's no way this plant just came inside me, I think, writhing in pleasure from the unfamiliar sensation. It feels so good that I grind into it, taking the phallus as deep as my sex will allow. *How is this even possible?*

"AH-AHH!" I cry out as a second jet of the liquid heat blasts directly into my cervical hole this time. As thickness gushes into me, flooding the organ behind my bladder, my pussy contracts around the spadix, gripping it like a fist holding onto a pullup bar for dear life, and this time it doesn't relax…

My limbs feel like noodles so, even if I wanted to shimmy back until this thing slides out of me, I can't. All I can do is lie here, squirming restlessly. The unyielding orgasm has my immobilized body trembling while the plant pulsates inside of my still clenched cavity like the heart of a running cheetah, each throb pumping a viscous geyser of what feels like warm honey straight into my womb. To have that toasty thickness spreading across the untouched regions of my uterus, feeling that flesh chamber expand as it's flooded with this plants *ejaculate*—it's one of the best things I've ever felt, and it makes me come all over again.

As the pressure of the viscous jet finally wanes after the fourth blast, the spadix suddenly swells inside my vagina like a rapidly expanding water balloon, stretching me almost like that too-wide eggplant that I forced into my tight hole a few weeks back. And, as it somehow becomes more and more engorged by the second, there's suddenly a strange tickling sensation that quickly moves from inside my cervical hole to deep inside my womb.

Having stickiness dripping deep inside of me is probably what's tickling me, I think, trying to make sense of what I'm feeling.

That's when something that feels like multiple thin noodles begins dragging across my uterine walls. At that moment, the image of those clear vines that I saw coming out of the plant's sap hole pops into my mind. Now I'm imagining that the plant's *ejaculate* carried the vines through my cervix and into my womb. Whatever the case may be, the foreign sensation feels too fucking good to worry about.

The pressure from having the plant's phallus still expanding inside of me doesn't feel as pleasurable anymore. Being stretched like that is actually starting to feel really uncomfortable.

How is this fucking plant still swelling? With all the syrupy goodness it pumped into me, it should be shriveling up from having nothing left.

I squeeze my abdominal muscles and push like I'm trying to give birth but, even as lubed up as it is, the plant doesn't launch out of me the way bananas, cucumbers, and eggplants do when I Kegel like this.

Guess I have to pull it out…

I don't know if I'm drained from the orgasm or if this sap contains a sedative, but blissful drowsiness suddenly washes over me and I feel extremely sedated. It takes everything in me to lift my arm and reach between my legs. When my fingers meet the inch or so of the spadix that's not buried in my still clenched cunt, I'm shocked to find that it's twice as wide around as it was before.

I can't even wrap my hand all the way around it anymore… Not only is it girthier, but the petals that once formed a tight, narrow skirt around the stalk now feels like they have become more rigid and unfurled a bit. *What the hell? It's blossoming inside of me?*

"This skirted arum flower is full of surprises," I whisper sleepily as I curl my pointer and thumb around the apple-wide shaft right behind where the petals are growing out of it.

Not only is the spadix wedged against my still clenched vagina's walls, but the slickness that gushed out and coated the plant makes it too slippery to grip. Every time I try pulling it out, my hand glides off of it. Since I don't want to hurt the flower by squeezing it too hard, I instead opt to reach down with both hands to see if I can pinch it by the firm petals and pull it out that way.

Except, when I start tugging, it barely moves half a centimeter before it stops budging. And when I pull harder, fear of ripping off the albeit sturdy petals makes me give up. Because I don't want it out of me bad enough that I'm willing to damage this marvelous plant.

It's not like I don't stuff my cunt full of leaves, veggies, and fruit for hours at a time on a regular day, so if I don't get it out right away that won't be the worst thing in the world.

My finger traces the *slit* between where my taut labia and the engorged spadix meet. When I try slipping my finger between them to see if I can pull myself open wide enough to maybe help push the spadix out, I can't even slide it in a little. Not only is the grip my pussy has on the phallus way too tight, but there's some squishy gunk that feels like chewed gum adhering my flesh to the plant.

"Hmm…" *Maybe I can pull it by the stalk…*

My fingers caress their way down a stiff petal that now feels like a thin, flexed muscle. Just as my digits slip between the gap between the petals, there's a loud squish of a pop and I feel the girthy stalk slap against my fingers as it's ejected from the flower's center like a hot dog out of a canon.

Using what little strength I can muster, I brush the auburn hairs from my face then I fight against the intensifying drowsiness to force myself to sit up and look down between my spread legs. Jutting out of the soil between my thighs is the now limp, wrinkled white stalk. It's bent towards me and there is an off-white, creamy sludge oozing out of the wide hole in the center of it.

So, the stalk shriveled but the spadix and petals plumped up?

The length of the stalk doesn't seem right. It's somehow still almost three-quarters of the plant's full height from the base of the stalk to where the tip of the spadix was even though the rest of the plant is still in me.

It's almost like it ejected its entire core to hollow itself out, which means there should be a deep hole that leads from the flower's center to the opening in the spadix's crown…

Now I look down at the flower sticking out of me. All but one inch of the eight-inch-long spadix is exposed from my splayed open pussy. The brown and pink meaty curtains of my inner labia are each clung against a separate petal and, when I try to lift my vaginal lips off of them, they don't budge.

It's like they're glued to the petals with the dried sap…

At the base of the spadix, the waxy, pale petals are gaped open like the starfish-shaped mouth of some monster. It's freaky looking, but it looks like a flower is sprouting out of my coochie and, as an Ecosexual, that's a huge turn-on for me.

As I slip my fingers between two of the five partially blossomed petals, I don't find the rest of the stalk, as expected. Instead, my middle finger pushes right into a humid, slimy, fleshy hole at the flower's center. The tubular cavity that my digit glides into feels just as soft and slick inside as the underside of the petals, and it's so tight that it hugs my skinny finger with the kind of pressure that'd likely make a man cum in two strokes.

Gosh, it feels like I'm fingering another woman—a woman whose pussy is tight like a slightly relaxed butthole filled with aloe vera slime… A moan escapes me.

As I plunge my finger deeper into the vagina-like hole in the center of the petals to see how deep it goes, three fleshy petals close around my hand like a starfish trying to hug me. Considering that I'm knuckle deep and the top of my palm is mashed against where the petals converge, this squishy hole must go all the way into the middle of the phallus that's swollen inside of me. Hell, it probably goes all the way to the opening pressed against my cervix.

Upon pulling my finger out of the flower's tightness, I find that my digit is not only completely covered with that same mayonnaise-like goo I saw oozing out of the stalk, but it's also glazed with a clear coating of yellow sap. Since there's no way all of that sap and white gunk came out of the spadix, there has to be another part of the flower underground where all of this fluid was stored.

Since I already licked up the first secretion this plant oozed out, I figure why not taste the new goo. So, as I lay back down, I suck the stuff I just fingered out of this plant's new hole off of my finger. The honey and candied cherry-flavored sap coating the outside quickly gives way to this very earthy, gritty, and sort of bitter paste. I don't hate it, but I don't love it either.

As my tongue slithers around my middle finger to clean off the rest of the bland gunk plastered on my digit like cake icing, the discomfort from being stretched out by an engorged plant diminishes a bit. It doesn't feel like the spadix has deflated at all, but it does feel like my vaginal walls are finally relaxing around the phallus. And now that I'm not uncomfortable anymore, the thought of being stuffed with a cock-shaped plant that's plugging me up with all of that sap and cream makes me horny all over again.

So, instead of attempting to pull this swollen spadix out of my cavity, I just lay here atop the mound of soil with my eyes closed, rubbing my clit to the memory of the beautiful sexual experience I just shared with this phallic flower.

Minutes later, I go from delicately rubbing my needy little nub to just lying there with my fingers resting on my pubic mound as I begin dozing off. And, just as sleep is taking hold, every inch of flesh inside my pussy begins to tingle…

CHAPTER 3
A FLOWER STUCK INSIDE ME

Saturday

This vaginal tingling sort of feels like what I'd imagine it'd be like having a pussy filled with warm vinegar and baking soda. The pleasant torture of internal fizzing makes me involuntarily Kegel around the plant's phallus, but the adrenaline-fueled panic over the concerning sensation prompts me to sit up. When I look between my legs, I find that the coating of yellowish sap between the base of the spadix and the beginning of the petals has become a crystalized glaze.

Since it's not slick with sap anymore, maybe I can pull it out of me, I think, curling my pointer and thumb around the bit of phallus protruding from my cunt.

Even though my hand doesn't slip off, and despite the fact the cock-shaped spadix inside of me has finally deflated a bit, it doesn't budge. Not even a little…

Maybe if I stand up, that'll help, I think, shifting onto my hip and planting my palms in the spongy soil.

Holding my skirt up to my belly, I climb to my feet, watching below as the still-warm flower petals dangling from my snatch slap against my inner thigh with sticky claps. Barely a second after standing, something that looks like white yogurt with a tinge of pale-yellow gushes out from the hole between the petals with a bubbly spurt, sending globs of goo splashing into the puddle of clear sap below. With the same hand keeping my skirt hiked up, I reach down and grab three petals then lift them so I can better see what's leaking out of the flower. A second later, the tingling inside makes my pussy flutter repeatedly like a heartbeat. Each involuntary Kegel squeezes the phallus stuffed inside my cavity, forcing more of the plant's *ejaculate* out of the flower's opening with bubbly spurts. As the seconds tick by, a few drips of white goo become a stream of creamy leakage.

It looks like I'm coming pudding…

After maybe a minute of watching interspersed yogurt-like streams turn into more of a melted white cheddar texture, clear yellow sap pours out of the flower's opening. As soon as the syrup stream thins into a trickle, I plunge a finger up into the flower's pussy-like hole then I stretch the fleshy tube open so I can finger out more of the sap and goo.

After sucking the deliciousness off of my finger, I squat a bit then I pull down on the phallic plant harder than I ever did before. Despite being rougher with it this time around, there isn't even the slightest sensation of the spadix sliding against my vaginal walls. However, as I'm tugging the plant downward, it does feel like the once slippery phallus is now pulling every inch of flesh in contact with the spadix, including the tender flesh of my cervix…

Um, why does it feel like the spadix has been hot-glued to my inner walls? I tug a bit harder.

"Ah!" I scream, snatching my hand from the flower. "Holy shit… it's, like, *really* fucking stuck inside me…" I whisper in disbelief. "Oh, fuck… Fuck, fuck… What did I do?"

The sap must've turned into glue before it hardened… I look down at the liquid I spent several minutes watching gush out of the flower before my gaze wanders to the yellowish sap puddled around the base of the limp stalk. *But wait… if there is still liquid sap coming from deep inside the spadix, why did the secretions between the plant's phallus and my vagina turn into glue? And why didn't the sap and gunk that I swallowed make glue my throat shut?*

"Maybe it reacted with something in my vaginal juices…" I whisper.

To keep from panicking, I close my eyes, take a deep breath, and exhale nice and slowly. *Think of a solution… Think of a solution… Solution… Solvent solution…*

The slickness that came out of the skirted arum plant was sweet and sticky, which means there's sugar in it. Maple syrup contains sucrose from the xylem sap of the tree, that's why the spout on maple syrup bottles gets sticky and hard when it dries out. But it will dissolve in water over time… All I have to do is hike back to that river I passed on the way here and sit in the water until this sap dissolves.

"But before I leave here…" I say quietly, letting my skirt down before kneeling beside the goo puddle and reaching for the limp white stalk.

The veiny stem feels like a giant, overcooked asparagus when I grip it, and it's warm like one too. *No, better yet, it feels like a limp dick wrapped in a waxy banana leaf.* The thought makes me snicker.

There's one wide hole in the stalk's center and two narrower ones on either side and, when I squeeze the flaccid thing, white sludge swirled with tan and yellow streaks oozes out of them.

Where is this stuff coming from? There's got to be another part of it underground…

Holding the limp stem with three fingers, I use my free hand to brush away the soil around the base. Eventually, I uncover another three inches of the stalk as well some kind of small sac that looks like it has testicles inside of it…

Ah, so that's where you've been hiding your fruits, I think, fondling the leathery sac.

The balls inside are about the size of concord grapes and they're about as squishy as lychee. During my attempt to find a way to get the fruits or seeds out of the thin membrane, I accidentally tear the sac away from the stalk, ripping a hole the size of my thumbnail in the fleshy pouch. Using my phone's flashlight, I look inside and find two white, opaque, oval balls that look just like lychee.

Scratch that, they look like actual testicles… Of course, a penis-shaped flower has two fruits in a leafy scrotum that looks exactly like a man's balls, I think, grinning and shaking my head. Curious as to what they taste like, I stick my tongue in the sac's hole and give the one I pushed toward the center a lick. The squishy ball feels rubbery like calamari against the tip of my tongue, and it doesn't taste the least bit sweet at all. It's just bland. *Doesn't taste like fruit… I wonder what would happen if I planted these in my backyard… Would they sprout a new skirted dick flower? Only one way to find out…*

After grabbing the collapsible silicone bowl from my backpack, I gently tear away the *scrotal* tissue from the stalk. Once the membrane is removed, I find that the rubbery balls are attached to the stalk with thin, fleshy cords. It doesn't take much effort to rip the first one away from the withered stem. As soon as I yank the second one free, I place both balls back in the sac then place them in the dish for safekeeping.

With the scrotum-like fruit pouch is safely tucked away in my backpack, I continue brushing away more of the soil beneath the stalk. Right beneath where the *ball sac* was, I uncover another inch of stalk before finding the bottom of the plant. Well, not really the *bottom*. At least, I don't think it is, because it's connected to something bizarre. There aren't any roots—at least not in the traditional sense. Growing down and out from the base of the underground portion of the stalk are dozens of fleshy, white cords that branch into skinny white threads resembling mushroom mycelium.

These threads look just like what came out of the phallus's tip…

There are also pale, pink veins on either side that are thick like arteries. Both types of *roots* are webbed across a squishy mass that has the color and texture of slimy oatmeal that's been left out to harden for a few hours, forming fleshy skin.

It looks like a slime mold made of creamy oatmeal…

And the smell that wafts up from the hole I've dug? It's earthy, a bit floral, and kind of musty with faint putrid notes…

My nose curls and I retch. "What the fuck is this…" I gasp, poking it with a finger.

The subterranean mass feels exactly like I'm pressing into someone's flabby belly, and it freaks me the hell out. As I continue pressing harder into the surprisingly tough yet squishy rind, my finger pokes something hard beneath the surface that makes me snatch my hand away.

"Eww!"

It was like pressing into an overweight body and hitting bone… It was probably just a root or something though, I think, flattening my palm against the fleshy rind.

As I press down hard on what feels like a waterbed filled with mud, this white paste with amber streaks erupts out of the flaccid stalk like a snake spewing puss and sewage. And, of course, the gunk sprays all over my hand…

I spring up to my feet and back away from the stalk. "Oh gawd…" I retch. "Why's it so warm?" That's when a horrific realization hits me. "Whatever the flower ejaculated into me came from this gross pod or whatever it is…" The thought of my womb and vagina being pumped full of this filth makes me gag, but I somehow keep myself from puking.

How far does this squishy, underground pod go? I scan the dirt mound I'm standing on as I walk backward off of it, the petals between my legs slapping my inner thighs with each step. *God walking around with my pussy this stuffed is worse than the time I spent a day with Bok Choy stuffed up there… But at least the spadix's swelling is going down.*

It's only now that I'm not enthralled by the plant that I notice that the stalk isn't jutting out of the dead center of the mound like I thought, but, longways, it's actually closer to one end than the other—about the distance a penis would be from a man's feet if his body was the length of this mound… Also, the sac just so happened to be on the side of the stalk that's closer to the *bottom* end, like testicles under the shaft of a cock.

"How bizarre…" I whisper, eyeing the bulge in the earth before me. "Hmm…"

The oval dirt mound is about six feet long, almost two feet across. It's also about six inches higher than the rest of the soil in this clearing… Since it's the only mound as far as I can see, it's safe to assume that this pod or whatever probably spans the entire bulge of soil… And, even though there are no tree roots inside this hollow, I doubt the mass reaches the walls of the trunk.

To test my hypothesis, I kneel just 'south' of the stalk—south being the side of the mound lengthwise that the stalk is closest to—then I dig a small hole until my finger bumps something squishy beneath the soil. When I brush away a bit more dirt, I uncover more roots webbed across the gross, flabby encasing. The same thing happens when I dig a hole at the top of the mound by the opposing bark wall. And when I kneel with my back to either entrance to the hollow to dig holes left and right of the mound, it's no different. But when I go a foot away from each of the four holes and dig six inches deep, I find nothing.

There aren't even tree roots this far from the mound, which is odd considering I dug holes close to the bark walls inside this hollow trunk…

The curious, nature-loving botanist in me desperately wants me to clear the entire mound of soil away so I can uncover the entirety of whatever this flabby mass is that lies beneath.

I wanna uncover it, cut it open, and find out what's inside, then I want to take samples back home with me so I can get it tested by Julie over at the University of Washington...

The thought crosses my mind that I might not be able to navigate back here since I've wandered over three miles through the dense rainforest from the Hoh River trail to get here.

"Screw it... I'm digging it up while I'm here, otherwise, I'll wonder about it forever..."

I drop onto my knees before the hole at the 'southern' end of the limp stem. It's at that moment that I realize the tingling in my vagina has faded significantly. It's faded, but there is a new sensation spreading from where the plant's phallus is pressed against my cervix and all the way down toward my labia.

"Ah... Ugh... Why does my vagina feel so hot?" Well, maybe not hot, but it's warm, like a well-hung guy with fever just stuffed me with his toasty cock.

Temperature change is the sign of a chemical reaction, I think, hiking up my skirt and wrapping my hand around the exposed portion of the flower's phallus. To my surprise, the spadix has shrunken back to its original size at some point while I was digging holes. Still, when I tug it down with moderate force, it doesn't slide out even a little. *The fizzy tingling that I was feeling for the last twenty minutes or so was also likely a sign of a chemical reaction,* I think, squeezing the plant harder than ever before and yanking it downward with a bit more strength.

It still doesn't budge; it just pulls my inner flesh so hard that I cry out in pain. "AAAHH-HAAA-HA-AH!" It takes a moment to regain my composure after that. "Alright," I huff, panting afterward. "I think I need to get to the river right the fuck now." I start kicking the soil that I dug up back into the hole before me. "Once I get this flower out of my vagina, I'm going to grab the shovel from my tent, and then I'm coming back here to find out what you are," I say to the soil mound.

After quickly filling back in all of the holes, I pick up my panties and my cell phone, grab my backpack from the entrance to the hollow, then I race across the clearing. As though I'm running from a forest monster, I charge through the brush, moving hastily in the direction of the sound of the waterfall while the petals dangling out of my coochie slap loudly against my thighs.

The fever inside my vagina gets warmer and warmer with each passing minute.

Gradually, the fizzy tingling returns more intense than before.

Panic sets in and my heart races. *Oh god… what's happening down there?*

CHAPTER 4
SLOUGH

Saturday

Since soaking in the creek at the mouth of the waterfall's pond didn't help dissolve the adhesive in a timely matter, I decided to give up and hurry my ass back to the river by my campsite before sunset. That way, if soaking in the river winds up not helping and things happen to get worse *down there,* I'd at least be close by the ranger station.

About halfway through the three-mile speed walk through dense, mossy forest, the temperature inside my spadix-stuffed coochie seems to have stopped heating up, leveling off to what feels like the temperature of a hot water bladder. It's very warm and, while it's quite uncomfortable, it's not like it's burning or anything. Also, the fizzy, tingling feeling has waned once again. For now.

This entire hike, my mind has been racing—scrambling to figure out why a plant that's the perfect shape for a woman's vagina would basically glue itself inside of a mammal's genitals only to detach from its stalk and leave with her. It makes even less sense considering I ingested both secretions and neither my mouth nor throat were glued shut. I try to figure out why that would happen and why it's making my pussy tingle and increase in temperature.

There are two explanations that I come up with:

One: like the Monotropa uniflora—or the ghost pipe plant—the skirted arum plant that I decided to fuck was completely void of the green, phototropic cells needed for photosynthesis. And, since chlorophyll-lacking plants are often parasites who steal nutrients from a network of fungi who, in turn, steal sustenance from other plants, it's safe to assume that the skirted phallic flower growing in the dark hollow of a giant spruce was drawing energy from that gross, body temperature pod underground. Because if there's heat, there's energy.

But the pod didn't seem like a fungus that the flower was living off of, the underground mass seemed to be a part of it—like a gross taproot where it stored its sap and whatever that white and brown stuff it ejaculated into me...

So, if it's not a parasitic plant, there's a chance that it's likely just carnivorous. Carnivorous plants like the pitcher plant and Heliamphora use their nectar's sweet scent to lure in insects and small vertebrates, then the smooth wax lining the cupped leaf makes the prey slip into a pool of digestive enzymes that converts them into a solution of amino acids, peptides, ammonium, and urea. But the weird thing about the skirted phallic arum inside of me is that the petals were growing downward, so it's not like an insect would feed on the sap gushing up from the bulbous tip then fall into the petals where it would get trapped. Also, the underside of its leaves was colorful, not the outside. That's counterintuitive to a plant that wants to attract bugs...

What sort of prey would a plant shaped exactly like a cock need?

A vagina of course. A human vagina, because what other animal would try to mate with a plant other than a perverse woman?

The more I think about it, the more it makes sense. I mean, I was without a doubt lured to that plant by its intoxicating scent, and I started getting aroused before I even saw the thing. The second I stroked it, it throbbed and lubed itself like it was making itself ready for *intercourse*. And as soon as I started fucking it, it swelled up inside of me like it was trying to keep itself embedded in my pussy. Then it ejaculated warm jets of hot cream into me, flooding my cavity—a cream that likely caused my pussy to contract and cramp around it like a vice right after. It expanded in me at the same time my sex clamped around it, and by the time I tried pulling it out, the sap and goo rapidly catalyzed into an adhesive that basically glued it to my flesh…

On top of all of that, the flower ejected its stem from the core of the phallus as though it no longer wanted to be attached to the underground pod filled with slimy nutrients. It no longer needed to be attached to the stalk because it wanted to leave inside of the sex organ it was made to live inside of…

Does that mean my vagina is tingling and warming up because digestive enzymes are liquefying my flesh so it can feed off of me, its new host?

"Oh fuck," I whisper, going from powerwalking to jogging as the horrific realization makes my heart jackhammer in my chest.

After running the last three-quarters of the third and final mile, I stumble downhill then barrel through the brush onto the trail. From there, it's only a short walk to the secluded river that's a few yards off of the trail.

I move through the dense bushes and weave through the fern-covered trees until I reach the squishy bed of moss that leads to the river. There was no one on the trail just now, and I can't see anyone in the woods around me, so I drop my backpack against the tree, pull my dress over my head then set it on top of my pack. Looking down past my small breasts, I stare at the five starfish arm petals dangling out of my vagina. Even after being detached from the stalk, they don't look shriveled or withered at all. In fact, when I touch them, they're still pretty firm, and the pink, fleshy underside of the petals is still damp and warm to the touch—the same temperature as my skin. The hole at the center of the flower feels even warmer than before when I finger it. And when I pull my finger out from under the petals, it's slick with a milky slime speckled with tiny, pink chunks in it.

I suck my finger clean with a smack. "Tastes like…" I smack my lips again. "Tastes like a slightly sweeter version of my normal vaginal secretions, but with a tinge of bitterness…"

Without further ado, I step into the cold water, sloshing my way through the river until I'm knee-deep in it. That's when I squat down into the rushing waters, shivering as I sit my bare ass on a smooth, flat rock. I'm facing the direction of the current with my legs spread wide so that the force of the river can flow right into the flower's hole. Seconds after doing so, cold water finds its way to my feverish cervix, and damn does it feel so fucking good.

The minutes creep by. I've been sitting in the river for so long now that my fingers are pruning and my body temperature is starting to drop. When I sat down, the sun was just above the tree line. Now it has disappeared behind the towering trees and the sky is taking on the orange, purplish tinge of evening. To my best estimation, I've been sitting here like this for maybe thirty or forty minutes. Even though I've been soaking for that long, the fever in my vagina seems to have gone down a bit, but it's still noticeably warm and a little tingly in there.

More bad news: Even after all this time, I still can't even peel my pussy lips off of the petals, nor can I pull this thing out of me.

The water is definitely filling the flower's canal because my cervix feels nice and cool, but the water doesn't seem to be getting between the spadix and my vaginal walls at all… Even if it was, it probably wouldn't make a difference since I can't peel my labia off of the petals…

"This water isn't doing shit to dissolve this flower's adhesive…"

The crazy thing is, when I lift the petals and finger the flower's flooded canal, it's still warm to the touch and it still feels slick despite being full of cold water.

If it's still slick while filled with water, the lubrication is hydrophobic. But how is this flower still so warm inside? It should be cooling off…

"Fuck!" I shout, my jaw trembling. A sigh escapes me as I look to the sky.

It's going to be dark soon, so I better get back to camp…

After surveying the area and deeming that it's clear of people, I rise from the river and slosh my way back to shore. With every stride, water pours out of my flower in spurts. When I get to my backpack, I fish out my towel and my fleece jacket, then quickly dry myself off. Once my sundress is back on, I put on my fleece and zip it up to my chin.

My campsite isn't in the official campgrounds but hidden in a beautiful, mossy, fern-covered wonderland that's nestled in a clearing with a stream about a quarter-mile from the trail—a mile from the part of the river I just chose to soak in.

My body is shivering during the entire walk, and I'm starting to get really drowsy—drowsier than I was after the plant splooged in me. The longer I hike, the sleepier I get, the more of a struggle it is to walk, and the colder I feel, despite wearing this warm jacket and sweating.

By the time I spot my tent through the pair of Douglas fir trees, I feel like I'm about to pass out, and I'm not sure if that's because I haven't eaten a real meal since I left here around noon or if it's because this plant stuffed inside my cooter is doing something to me.

As soon as I get a fire going, I shed my sundress and put on a long sleeve shirt and a pair of sweatpants. It probably goes without saying, but it's a bitch putting on pants when you have five hand-sized *leaves* that are as thick as chicken cutlets hanging out of your vagina. The petals keep bunching up in the crotch of the pants so I have to tuck the ones on the left and right into the corresponding pant legs then I lift the one in front up towards my belly button and tuck it in the waistband the way guys do with boners they're trying to hide.

That'll do, I think, shivering as I put my fleece back on.

While I warm myself by the fire, I use the hot water I just boiled to rehydrate the last of my Mountain House chicken and mashed potato entrees. Even while I eat all layered up by the fire, I still feel really cold.

Not cold, feverish, I think, touching the back of my hand to the flesh between my neck and chin. *I'm definitely having a reaction of some kind to this plant. I don't know if the reaction in my vagina is giving me a low-grade fever or if this is the result of being poisoned from ingesting the sap…*

I sigh hard with an uneven, trembling breath. "Shit… I think I need to get to the hospital…"

Too bad I'm, like, ten miles from my car or the ranger station. And I barely have it in me to stand, never mind hike that far in the middle of the night…

I check my phone. "And, of course, I still don't have service this deep in the forest."

I don't have a choice but to sleep it off, I think, rising from the log that I've been using as a seat.

Upon disposing of my empty food pouch in the waste bag that I've hung from a tree a few feet away from camp, I crawl into my tent, zip it shut, and worm my way into my sleeping bag. In a matter of seconds, I start dozing off.

Painful cramping in my womb wakes me in the dead of night. As my eyelids snap open, my vagina throbs with a sharp cramp that's accompanied by this bubbly, squirt noise between my legs. It legit sounds like the flower stuffed inside me just sharted…

"Ah-oooh," I groan as I sit up with my hand pressed against the base of my belly. "What the shit…"

It's only after the wave of pain passes that I realize the fever is pretty much gone and my body is drenched in a cold sweat. As I shift in my sleeping bag, I feel something thick and cold squishing between my thighs. Whatever it is, it feels jelly, so I know the crotch of my sweats isn't drenched from the cold sweat...

During my shimmy out of the sleeping bag, my uterus cramps hard again, then my vagina cramps right after, making me double over in pain. "Ahhh!" And just like last time, the vaginal contraction is followed by a bubbly, squirt. After clicking on the battery-powered lantern beside my bedding, I lift my ass off of the ground and yank my sweatpants down, my eyes immediately widening in horror at the sight. "What the fuuuck..."

The large petals sticking out of my pussy are blossomed, unfurled like an opened hand with its fingers slightly curled inward. And when I pull the stiff and very warm petal that's right beneath my clit up and to the side, I find a gelatinous mass of what I can only describe as pink mashed potatoes mixed with chunks of red Jell-O clumped up between my thighs...

It looks like that time I had that weird period where my endometrium sloughed off in one big chunk... It resembles that, but it's pink like the flesh of my vagina and not a dark, bloody red...

"Oh my fuck... Is this... is this liquified uterine and vaginal flesh?"

As those words leave my mouth, my uterus cramps hard again, followed by another painful vaginal contraction. At the same time, the petal pinched between my pointer and thumb flexes hard as the flower blossoms. With a bubbly spurt, slimy pink chunks gush out from the flower's hole like vomit.

The sight makes me gag hard. "That's so fucking gross..." The musky, fleshy, slightly metallic, and floral smell that wafts up into my nose makes me gag even harder. "It even smells sort of like menstruation..."

In a fit of panicked desperation, I grip the flower then pull the warm, gently throbbing thing as hard as I can. Just like the last few times I attempted yanking this plant out, it doesn't budge, it just pulls my inner flesh so hard that my eyes water and I fold over in pain.

Sobbing, I just sit there in defeat, staring at the chunky stuff still being excreted from my flower's hole. As grossed out as I am, I'm curious to know if it tastes like me or if it tastes like the plant, so I stick my finger into the jiggling, gelatinous glob and bring the pinkish chunks with flecks of deep red to my mouth. Reluctantly, I scrape the gunk off of my fingers with my bottom row of teeth, letting the warm stuff splat onto my tongue. Whatever this stuff is, it has the thickness and texture of cottage cheese. And it tastes just like it smells—it tastes like someone chewed up a flower with a bit of honey, some pork, and a few drops of blood, then spit it onto my tongue… The consistency is like a mix between gritty mashed potatoes and gelatinous cranberry sauce.

"Bleh," I gag, spitting the gunk right back onto the horror scene between my legs. It takes everything in me not to hurl.

The cramping and oozing of pink gunk from my pussy's flower comes in waves that ripple through me at shorter and shorter intervals. For thirty long minutes, I sit there crying in my tent with my legs spread, watching the filth being ejected. And on that thirty-fifth minute, there's one really hard cramp that squeezes out the smallest volume of gunk I've seen thus far.

With that last painful contraction, the flower petals all suddenly relax and go limp. After no more cramps follow in the ten minutes that I spend staring between my legs, I decide that whatever was happening is done.

Thank God that's over, I think, grabbing the empty plastic food container from my backpack. Now I begin scooping up the mess in my sweatpants and the gunk on the floor of my tent into the Tupperware.

Once all the flower's excrement is cleaned up, I emerge from my tent into the cool night air and rinse off the flower's still warm petals with some water. Then I shove the nozzle of my sports bottle up into the flower's hole and squeeze a jet of water inside, blasting my cervix. Except the water doesn't stop at the cervix, it goes much deeper than that as though I'm dilated or something…

When I pull the nozzle out, water rushes out along with a few chunks. It takes two more rounds of douching for the water to come out chunk-free. Just to make sure the flower's canal is clean, I finger the tight, hot hole in the center of the petals and feel around. Satisfied that no more bits are coming out, I pull on a pair of backup sweats then crawl back into my tent.

"I can't believe all of this is happing to me," I whisper as I crawl back into my sleeping bag. "If I ever get this flower out of my vagina, I will never again fuck any weird-ass plants or mushrooms that I can't identify… I promise…"

I shut my eyes and try my best to think about anything other than what I went through today or what I just watched being expelled from between my legs.

CHAPTER 5
PART OF ME

Sunday

The second I open my eyes I'm blinded by the glare shining through the white fabric of my tent.

I groan. "Why is it so damn bright?" I say with a groggy voice, peeking through one eye at my Garmin watch. "What? How is it already 12:45 P.M.?" I spring up from my bedding. "I never sleep in this late..." Of the four days I've spent camping out here, I always got up around first light. Even when I'm on vacation, I only ever sleep until maybe 9:00 A.M.

I guess I did sort of wake up in the middle of the night to deal with that weird cramping from my flower's goo expulsion... And I guess it did take me a bit to fall back asleep afterward, but I shouldn't have slept in this long.

"Speaking of my flower..." I whisper as I scooch back out of my sleeping bag, staring curiously down at my crotch when I realize there's no tingling, warmth, or even pressure inside my vagina anymore. "Did it finally drop out of me in the middle of the night?"

As I'm pulling down my sweats, the fabric tickles what feels like my pussy lips. It feels so good that I Kegel hard, and as my vaginal muscles clench, the crotch of my pants bulge with the blossoming petals.

I guess it is still in me… But why don't I feel stuffed anymore? And why did it feel like my labia just flexed?

When I pull my pants down to my thighs, I find that the flower is right where I last saw it, its fleshy petals partially blooming outward once they're free of my pants. It still doesn't look withered at all. In fact, the flower looks plump and full of life—a bit rosier than I remember, its once pale veins now a purplish red.

Maybe I can pull it out now that I don't really feel it inside of me anymore…

Just like I've done before, I curl my fingers around the bit of spadix between my pussy lips and just behind where the petals are growing out from it. "Ah!" I yelp, snatching my hand away.

I reacted that way because, the moment I touched it, it felt like I touched myself. Which doesn't make sense. Because my fingers were centimeters away from my stretched labia…

As soon as I work up the nerve to touch it again, I feel it instantly. The bizarre sensation makes my core spasm, which in turn makes the long petals between my legs blossom wide like a hand stretching its fingers. And I feel it. I feel each one move as though it wasn't the petals that splayed out like that—it feels like my labia just opened up and flexed…

"What the heck…" I gasp, reaching for the petal curling up towards my belly.

When my finger meets the veiny, beige 'skin' of the flower petal, a tickling sensation shoots up to my vagina and tingles its way through my body.

"No way…" Now I reach for the pointy, arrowhead tip of the petal and pinch it hard. "OUCH!" I cry out. "Fuck, it feels like I just pinched my labia… But… how?"

Looking back to where my labia are plastered onto the part of their respective petals, I notice that the light brown flesh curtains of my inner pussy lips no longer look like they're *clung* to the petals.

No, now it appears as though the petals have grown *over* my skin a bit, and I can't tell where my flesh ends and the petals begin.

It's not just glued to me anymore; it's fused to my skin…

Instead of pulling the petals back like I did yesterday, I flex my vagina as hard as I can and, in response, the petals straighten out like a flat starfish.

Did I just… Did I just control it?

I reach both hands underneath the flower and I lightly touch the vibrant pink underside of two different petals. When my fingers press into the warm, soft, wet, vagina-like squishiness, the petals twitch from my caress, sending surges of pleasure racing from the petals up into my vagina.

It feels like I just fingered myself, I think, trembling in sweet agony as I lightly trace my middle finger down the length of the petal's underside to the tight hole in the flower's center. When I slide my finger into the tight cavity and push all the way into the middle of what used to be the spadix, it feels exactly like I'm just slipping a finger into my vagina.

No, scratch that, I think, pulling my finger out of the tightness only to slide it back in even deeper than before, as deep as I can go. *It feels like I'm fingering a tighter, wetter, more hypersensitive version of my pussy even though I'm not even touching my pussy…*

"Or maybe I *am* touching my pussy," I moan, the flower's pussy hole squelching as I finger it hard and fast. *I'm feeling what the flower feels because it's not just stuck in me anymore, it's fused to my vagina. It's part of me…* "AHHHH! OOHH-AH!" I cry out as I'm blindsided by a climax.

As a mind-scrambling orgasm—as the best orgasm of my life ripples through my flower, my pussy, my womb, and then my body, the petals flex open wide only to close around my hand over and over with each pleasant contraction, the dripping petals hitting the skin on my arm and hand with wet, sticky slaps.

God this thing is so wet. No. Correction, the juices dripping from the petals and the hole are not just from it or me, it's from us. We are wet.

As I lay there drunk with pleasure, my body a limp mess of limbs, I think back to the tingling, the vaginal fever, and the sloughed off vagina and womb chunks that the cramps expelled from me last night.

The reason it doesn't feel like the spadix is stuffed inside of me anymore is that there is no spadix inside of me—the spadix has become one with my birth canal while the petals have essentially become extensions of my labia. The plant wasn't digesting my pussy so it could consume me for sustenance, it was liquifying itself and me so it could merge its flesh with mine, a symbiotic unification that allows it to draw nutrients directly from my blood rather than digesting me…

I look down at the petals as they're curling back into a relaxed state and drooping slowly between my legs like five leaf-shaped penises all losing their erections simultaneously.

The veins on the leafy petals have now gone from beige to the color of blood because they've connected to my vascular system. But it's not just its flesh and veins that fused with mine, but also its nerves—because what touches it, I feel.

While plants don't have neurons, this bizarre plant surely had some kind of nervous system prior to me screwing it, because it *did* react to touch with throbbing and sap gushing. Also, when I masturbated with the phallus to climax, it knew to ejaculate a secondary slime in me before swelling and locking itself inside my vagina after its cream made my vagina clench around it. Then, last night, without even being attached to the stalk, it flexed inside of my vagina on its own and throbbed inside of me like a heart all so it could spew that pink, mashed potato-looking stuff out of me. And that was before I started feeling whatever sensations the flower was feeling.

That means, at some point during the additional ten hours of sleep following the 1:30 A.M. cramps, its nerves rapidly merged with mine, allowing me to feel whatever pain and pleasure it sensed—allowing me to control when the petals open and close by flexing and relaxing my vaginal muscles.

"The flower is me and I am the flower," I say softly, smiling as I caress my way from my flower's puckered pussy hole along the slick underside of the petals and all the way up to the tip.

I'm smiling not just because tickling my hypersensitive vagina-flower feels amazing, I'm smiling because I'm incredibly happy that the flower is a part of my body now. I love plants so much, and now my sex organ has somehow unified with the most beautiful, most fascinating, most sexual-looking plant I've ever seen.

"I put a dick-shaped plant inside me and then it morphed into a part of my pussy… Wild…"

But how can a plant merge with an animal?

Between flora and fungi, fungi are the most similar to animal cells, that's why it's sometimes difficult to treat fungal infections without harming our cells—that's why ringworms and candida can grow in and on us.

I sit up and pet my petals, my core spasming from each gentle caress. "If this isn't a special plant that is somehow capable of fusing to human flesh, that means this thing that has grafted itself to my coochie isn't a parasitic or carnivorous plant at all…" I take off my fleece then I remove my long sleeve shirt. "That means it *is* a fungus that not only mimicked a flower's appearance to lure in prey, but it also mimicked human penis because it needed to find its way into a vagina so it could merge with it…"

The question is, why? Why does it need a vagina specifically? And how is this species even alive when most women of sound mind would never masturbate with an unknown, penis-shaped lifeform growing out of the ground?

The image of the squishy, tapioca pudding-like mass webbed in veins that I uncovered beneath the soil the mound flashes in my mind.

That pod-mass must have contained a store of nutrients that it stole from nearby plants and fungus in the area to sustain itself while it remained dormant for centuries or possibly eons, waiting until someone like me came along, got aroused by its pheromones, and decided to have sex with it… Maybe that's why nothing was growing in the clearing around the tree hollow, not even moss—and this forest is covered in the stuff…

After pulling on the sundress that I had on yesterday, I give my petals an over the skirt rub. "Are you the only one of your kind? Will another one of you sprout from those little fruit things that were growing inside your sac?" During my crawl out of the tent, the sensation of my dress brushing against the petals makes the flower throb and blossom between my legs.

Guess I'm going to have to get used to things touching my sensitive flower… And I'm going to have to get used to these petals slapping the inside of my legs for the rest of my life…

For breakfast, I have oatmeal, which is unfortunate that this is the only breakfast I have left because all I can think about as I chew the mush is the disgusting pod that looked like what I'm eating…

Despite being grossed out by my meal, I devour it. I scarf it down because it's insanely sweet thanks to the obscene amount of brown sugar I mixed into it. Normally, I only put a teaspoon of sugar into my oats but, since I was *really* craving sugar today, I ended up dumping in the three or four tablespoons I still had left in the baggy.

As soon as I'm finished eating, I get to work taking down my shelter. It takes nearly thirty minutes to break down and pack away the tent. And once I get it all rolled up and attached to the underside of my backpack, I venture through the bush back to the trail.

Now that my vagina isn't burning and tingling anymore—now that I'm not feverish, I'm not really in a rush to go back home today. All I want to do is hike back to the clearing where I discovered this skirted dick flower so I can investigate the underground pod. Because I desperately need to know why the jets of goo that erupted from deep underground were so warm when anything under the soil should be cooler than my body temperature.

It's only after staring up at the sky that I decided against going back. Looks like there are rain clouds on the horizon rolling in from the west—the direction I need to hike to get out of the Hoh Rainforest.

The pod is over an hour in the opposite direction of my car. If I leave now and walk at a brisk pace, I might be able to hike the fifteen miles to the visitor center where I parked before it rains. If I go back to where the pod is, I'll probably get rained on before I even finish digging it up. Then I'll have a four-hour hike ahead of me in a rainstorm.

I'd also like to plant those testicle-looking fruits before they rot or dry out...

With a huff, I face left then start walking west. "Home it is then..."

That pod better still be intact when I venture back out here next weekend...

CHAPTER 6
CRAVINGS & GROWING PAINS

Sunday

An hour into my drive, I feel this tickling sensation deep inside of me, like there's something soft and fuzzy spreading from my cervix to where I imagine my fallopian tubes are. It tickles so bad that my abdomen reflexively twitches, and the sporadic spasms make my flower throb and blossom so hard that my dress flutters up like there's a twitching erection between my legs.

Geez, it really freaking itches in there, I think, pressing against the base of my belly with my fingers like that's somehow going to help.

In the time it takes for Red Hot Chili Peppers' *'Under the Bridge'* to start and end, the exit for the gas station appears ahead. Right as I'm turning onto the offramp, there's a flash of pain from my uterus from a cramp that comes out of nowhere. I flinch so hard from it that I double over and swerve onto the gravel-lined shoulder of the road for a few seconds before swerving back into my lane.

"And here I thought the cramps were done now that this thing fused to my vagina…" I groan, holding my belly.

Not long after pulling up to the red light, the pain fades only to be replaced by this weird sensation that sort of feels like the deepest part of my vagina is being stretched open ever so slowly as though there's a mini speculum prying open my cervix.

I don't know if women are capable of feeling themselves dilating before childbirth but, if we can, I imagine this is exactly what it feels like…

And as if the discomfort of dilating for no reason isn't enough, my cervix is also starting to tickle now.

Experiencing vaginal warmth and tingling in the moments after the phallus swelled in me, having painful cramps that expelled chunky jelly and made me think the flower was dissolving and eating me? That was terrifying. Waking up to discover that the flower grafted itself to the inside of my birth canal to become new, hypersensitive flesh that I could feel was something I could live with. But now that I'm getting cramps and feeling things happening inside of me again, I'm beginning to worry that I'm not out of the woods yet after all.

When I get home, I'm going to call Dr. Sloane and set up an OB/GYN checkup, because I trust her and I need to know what's happening inside of me… Unless things get worse, then I'll go to the ER…

The gas station I pull into is the only establishment on this side of the road—exactly what you'd expect from being in Middle-of-Nowhere, Washington. There are a few cars parked in front of the convenience store, but I'm the only car at the pumps. Since it's a quiet Sunday afternoon with several pumps available, I take a moment to text my friends now that I finally have service.

The first person I add to the group chat is Julie Bloom, one of my best friends from college who's currently getting her master's in genetics and molecular biology over at our alma mater, the University of Washington in Seattle. The second person I add is Priya Singh, my first roommate who became like a sister to me after only one semester together. Not only is Priya the first person I go to for everything, but she also happens to be a mycologist who works with mushrooms for a living out in Tacoma.

If there are any two people who can help me figure out what has fused to my lady parts, it's them. And even if they can't, they are the only souls I'm comfortable talking to about this.

Me to the group: **Hey, girls! Can you 2 meet me at the house in an hour? I know it's short notice, but it's a bit of an emergency… Not, like, I'm dying emergency, but yeah… And don't freak out if I don't respond to your texts in the next forty minutes or so, I'm just driving back from Olympic National Forest, I didn't die or anything haha.**

At least I better not be dead within the next hour, I think, wincing as I hit send.

My sights lock right onto the shelves stocked with sweets the second I walk into the gas station. Now all I can think about is stuffing my face with sugary goodness until I'm sick. I'm craving sugar so bad that I want to eat a pack of candy, a chocolate bar, and wash it all down with a Sprite.

Either all of these years on a low sugar diet is catching up with me or my new flower parts have me craving sugar… Either way, my body is trying to tell me something, so I won't ignore my urges.

I grab some Pop-tarts and gummy worms since I haven't had any of those in ages, then I make my way to the fridges.

The blonde woman in her mid-30s walking in my direction smiles at me. And, right after we pass each other, I hear her inhale deeply. "Oh wow!" she says, almost in a moan. "Excuse me."

I twirl around with a smile. "Yes?"

"What is that amazing fragrance you're wearing?" Her breasts heave as she inhales more of whatever she's smelling.

"I'm not wearing anything…" I say with a confused smile.

She leans in uncomfortably close and sniffs, squeezing her thighs together as she leans back. "You sure? Because it smells like someone doused you in exotic flower oils then dumped vanilla and mango all over you." She giggles. "I mean, wow! It's heavenly!"

Her description makes me think back to the scent in the forest that led me to the flower now growing out of my cooch. *I haven't really noticed the flower's fragrance since it got stuck in me… I guess it didn't fade, after all. I just got overstimulated by it and became nose blind.*

I laugh nervously. "You know what? I totally forgot that some lady I met at the end of the trail let me try some of the essential oils she was trying to sell. I wish I could remember the name of her store, but I can't! Sorry!"

"That's a shame, but no worries! If I ever found a perfume or oils that smell that exquisite, I'd probably wind up maxing out my credit cards on the stuff!"

She and I share a laugh, exchange a few more words, then we go our separate ways.

After grabbing a bottle of Sprite, I head to the counter and stand in line behind a middle-aged man who's standing behind that same woman. As if she smelled that I was behind her, she turns around with a bright smile before heading for the exit. That's when the guy who was between us approaches the register, tipping his chin up to the ceiling and sniffing around like a dog on his way to the counter.

When he hears the plastic candy bag rustle in my hand, he turns around, one hand blatantly adjusting his hard-to-miss erection. "Is that you that smells so gosh darn amazing?" he says, turning his crotch towards the counter to keep me from witnessing any more of whatever he's doing to his boner.

"Holy shit, that smells incredible!" the pimply-faced teenager behind the counter blurts out.

I grin. "Why, yes, it is me! Trying a new essential oil my friend is working on."

The man leans in and inhales deeply, then he jerks back like he didn't mean to get so close. "Shit… Well, tell your friend to stop working on it, because if she leaves it as is she'll be rich to the tits!" He lets out a bellowing laugh. "Whatever that is, it's intoxicating!"

"Thanks! I will let her know that!"

After the man pays for his beers and sandwich, the grinning guy gives me a nod, covers his crotch with his bag, then heads for the door only to stop abruptly. "Hey, this might be inappropriate, but would you want to grab a drink with me and maybe tell me about your friend's essential oil business? I'm looking to invest in a new project."

I try not to scowl. "Sorry, but I have somewhere I need to be."

He nods then steps outside.

That was weird, I think, approaching the counter, watching as the smiling cashier seemingly adjusts his manhood behind the counter too. *Wait, does this guy also have a boner?* I think back to how horny I got when I first smelled this flower. *Don't tell me that everyone who smells me is going to get horny from now on...*

CHAPTER 7
FLOWER REVEAL PARTY

Sunday

"Home sweet home," I sigh as I turn onto my driveway from the heavily wooded road.

My two-story home here at 9901 93rd Ln SE in Olympia, Washington is the last house at the end of this road, nestled in a dense enclave of trees with no neighbors for almost a quarter-mile. Two miles east of the property, there are miles and miles of forest. If you walk far enough, you'd hit my favorite local place to hike to and camp at, Fiander Lake—the place my parents would always take me when we used to visit grandpa here before he passed away, a spot where I still venture to most weekends if I've got nothing going on. Whether you go south, southwest, or southeast of my backyard, there is nothing but woods for about three miles, save for the small, unnamed body of water due south about a mile that all the kids call Yelm Lake. To the north, it's pretty much all farmland until you hit Yelm Highway.

Basically, thanks to my grandfather leaving this house to me, I live in the middle of nowhere and I love it—a welcomed change after living in Seattle during my college years.

All my camping stuff gets dumped in the garage, then I run upstairs to the bathroom because I really need to go number two. Before I sit on the potty, I drape my pussy petals over the toilet seat so they don't dip into the water. It's only just now dawning on me how difficult it's going to be to pee sitting down. If I lift my petals and set them on the toilet seat, the pee is going to run down the top leaf that's right beneath my urethra like a water slide. If I let them hang in the toilet, the two petals in-line with each booty cheek will be in the water…

Well, I guess I could pee standing up and use the top petal sticking out under my peephole to funnel the water in…

Once I'm done, I hop in the tub and take a nice, long, hot shower. The feeling of gentle water splattering against my sensitive petals has me moaning the entire time. Drying the outside of my petals with a towel tickles them just as much.

I slip on a green, knee-high sundress with pink dots, then I venture downstairs and grab the flower's leafy sac containing the lychee-like balls. After that, I pop into the shed to get a shovel before heading out to the woods behind my backyard. I only go a few yards into the small, shaded clearing—far enough that no one could see a cock-like plant growing in the woods if they were to stand right at the tree line, but not so far that it's off my property line. That's where I dig a six-inch deep hole that I fill right back up after plopping in one of the testicle-like fruit-thingies.

I really hope this works, I think, heading back to the house. *Then I can study the lifecycle of this plant without going back and forth to Hoh Rainforest…*

"Hello?" I hear a girl's voice call as soon as I walk through the back door.

"I'm in the kitchen, Priya!" I say, shutting the door behind me.

Priya's bare feet clap urgently against the wooden floor then the petite, five-foot-tall, brown-skinned beauty appears around the corner with a concerned smile, her curtain of black hair swaying just over her ass. "Hey-hey!" she singsongs, her hazel eyes looking over me worriedly as she sets her purse on the counter. She then opens her arms for a hug.

"Hey, girl!" I say as I embrace her.

"Holy moly!" she sniffs hard as she embraces me. "Fuck, you smell absolutely heavenly!" She pulls away only to lean back in and sniff me from head to tits. "You look like you just came out of the shower. New shampoo? New perfume? Whatever it is, I want it!"

"Nope…"

"Then what is that? I'm practically drooling right now."

"Weird question, but do you feel horny right now?"

She scowls, but her features soften a moment later. "Actually, yeah… I feel like I haven't gotten laid in years even though I just had sex last night. How did you know?"

"Had a hunch."

"Okay… As much as I want to ask you why your super-secret fragrance is turning me on, I really want to know what's going on with you. Is everything okay?"

My smile morphs into a wince. "Yes? Maybe? Honestly, I don't know."

Her eyes widen. "Allie… please tell me what's going on before you worry me sick…"

"I was hoping you and Julie would get here at the same time so I don't have to tell this story twice."

"Well, Julie texted saying that she was going to be, like, forty minutes behind, so please don't keep me waiting unless you want me to have a heart attack in your kitchen…"

I inhale deeply, hold my breath for a few moments, then I huff. "Okay… I need to show you something before I tell you." I pull up the pictures I took of the skirted phallus flower before I fucked it.

Priya's tan cheeks redden and she snickers. "What is this, photoshop? You texted me to come here to see your photo editing skills?"

Smirking, I shake my head. "Oh, it's *real*. It's a plant I found in the Hoh Rainforest yesterday."

"Really? I mean, I've seen phallic plants and phallic mushrooms, but none that looked *exactly* like a pasty man's erection." She cackles.

"Yeah, me either… And that's why you're not going to be surprised when I tell you what I did with this flower's spadix…"

"*Allie Hannigan*… You didn't."

"I did…"

She snickers. "*Allie*…"

"Priya, this smell that's got you all hopped up on horny hormones? Well, that's what led me to this plant growing in this tree's hollow. This intoxicating scent had me horny out of my mind. And when I stroked it to see what it felt like, it throbbed and coated itself in this sweet, slippery sap and—and I just couldn't help myself."

She shakes her head. "Geez… I mean, I guess I shouldn't be surprised. You do prefer to use cucumbers instead of dildos, and eggplants instead of actual penises, Ms. 'I'm-an-Ecosexual-and-have-a-Plant-Kink…'" she says with a smile and a wink.

"See, now I'm glad I told you that story in junior year of college. Now you've had two years to prepare for this story."

"Seriously. Okay, so… How was it?"

"It felt just like a cock, but maybe a bit leatherier, I guess? It was even warm like one…"

"A plant with a body temperature? Are you sure it wasn't a guy buried in the dirt with his schlong out?"

I laugh, shoving her shoulder playfully. "No, you goof! The plant just looked and felt like a cock. Oh, and the underside of its leaves? It was slick as an aloe leaf."

"No way…"

"Yes way. And when I came, it throbbed spurted all sorts of syrup and creamy stuff into me."

"Hold on, are you trying to tell me that a plant *ejaculated* in you?"

I give her a slow and dramatic nod.

"Well… did you bring it back for me to try?" she snickers. "Kidding! Please don't pull out your used dong-flower and plop it in my hands. That'll be a repeat of that time I was cleaning and found a *used* cucumber under your bed all over again."

I laugh nervously. "Yeah, I don't think you want any part of that."

Her eyes go wide. "Why, did you have an allergic reaction to it or something?"

"Not exactly…"

"Uh-oh… *Allie*…"

"I need to show you something—something in a very private place on my body."

"Oh god… do you have a weird rash on your yoni that you want me to see so I can tell you whether or not you need to go to the doctor?" Priya Singh is Hindi and, in Hinduism, the yoni is a representation of the vulva, vagina, and womb—a symbol for the gateway of divine reproductive energy often portrayed as circular stone. For as long as I've known her, she has only ever referred to vaginas as yonis, cooter, vajayjay, vadge, coochie, or vagine. Same thing with penises. She calls them anything other than the normal names. The funny thing is, she's not a virgin. Far from it.

"It's not a rash, but I do need you to take a look at my *yoni* if you don't mind…"

"It's not like I haven't seen you naked literally dozens of times in the two years we shared a dorm. So, go ahead and flash me."

I snicker. "Okay, but don't freak out…"

"What, are you swollen shut or something?"

"Or something…" I grab the bottom of my skirt. "Before I show you, just know that it's not as bad as it looks."

She takes a deep breath then slowly exhales. "Oh…kay…"

In one quick pull, I lift my skirt.

Her eyes widen in complete horror and fascination as she jumps back. "Holy fuck, it's stuck in you?"

"No, it's not stuck *in* me anymore. More like, the ejaculate made my pussy clamp around it, the spadix of the flower swelled up until it was too big to pull out, then it fused to my skin in the hours after it got stuck in me."

"Oh my gosh… You need to see a doctor so you can get it out before you get septic shock!"

"I think I'm alright on that front. The spadix didn't block me off, per se. There's actually a fleshy tube from the hole in the center of the flower that leads straight to my cervix. Here, look…" I hop up on the counter, scoot my ass back, and spread my legs wide, clenching my abdominal walls to bloom the flower.

Priya shrieks and jumps back again when the petals open like a creature with a starfish mouth. "Oh fuck! Did you just make it do that or did it do that on its own?"

"*I* did that."

"How?" she says, slowly reapproaching me.

"It didn't *just* fuse to me… It sort of became a part of me? Like, the fleshy tube in the flower that became exposed after the stem was ejected essentially replaced my vagina. And if I finger the flower's hole, it just feels like I'm diddling myself like normal, but more sensitive. Better, actually."

"I don't understand…"

I snicker. "Me either…"

"So, if I touch the outside or inside of the petals?"

"Then it'd feel like my labia are being touched."

"You're shitting me…"

I shake my head. "I shit you not… You know what? I'll close my eyes and you go ahead and touch my flower anywhere you want, then I'll tell you where you're touching me at."

"Allie…"

"Priya, just do it. Please. For science?"

Hesitantly, she reaches for the flower, my cue to cover my eyes with a hand. "And with this, we cross into a new level of friendship… Alright… Here I go…"

My body jumps from her touch and I feel my petals throb. "You're poking the outside tip of the one sticking out by the top of my left thigh."

"No way… How about now?"

A moan escapes me as she drags a finger across a petal. "Oooh… You're gently stroking the red side of the bottom right petal—the one that's sort of in-line with my right butt cheek."

"Correct again… How about—"

"Ow-ouch!" I yelp, removing my hands from my eyes. "You just pinched the tip of the one beneath my clit and urethra."

"Holy crap! Sorry! I had to know if it sensed pain too."

"It's okay, I did the same thing to myself this morning. I poked, I stroked, then I pinched it and screamed in my tent." I flash her a cringe of a smile.

"This is… insane and terrifying and incredible all at once…"

"You're telling me…"

"The petals are warm like flesh… And while the outside is a bit leathery, the pink underside really does feel like the inside of a yoni…" Priya rubs her pointer finger and thumb together. "And this lubricant… it feels just like coochie juice." She sniffs her fingers. "But it doesn't smell like cooch… It smells like a bowl of fruit in a field of flowers."

I snicker. "I never have to worry about feminine odor again!" We share a laugh.

"Lucky you!" she says after settling down.

"Priya, I want you to feel inside the tube."

Her eyes go wide, but there's a glimmer of excitement on her face. "You want me to *finger* your yoni? I mean your flower? I mean… your yoni flower's hole?"

"Yes, please finger my yoni flower." I snicker, then I cackle when the absurdity of that sentence hits me. "I really want you to get the grasp of exactly what I mean when I say the flower became my vagina."

"I guess I am pretty curious…"

"Then go on ahead. I promise it won't be weird."

"Okay then… Here we go…" Her hand disappears beneath my blossomed petals and my core spasms when her finger pushes through the slit and into the half-dollar-sized hole, slipping deep inside the tight passage that hugs her skinny finger. "Oh wow…" she gasps as her finger glides in past the middle knuckle. She nibbles at her bottom lip like she's getting turned on. "It feels like a super tight yoni! And it's so wet and slippery! I mean, wowza!"

"Right? Oh-ah—" When she unexpectedly pushes her digit as far as it can go, I cry out in ecstasy and Kegel, my yoni hole rhythmically squeezing and relaxing around her finger as she's trying to pull it out. That's when my petals clamp around her hand like a squid attacking a fish. "Sorry! Sorry!" I moan, trying to get my petals and my narrow cavity to relax.

As soon as the flower between my legs blossoms, she drags her finger out with a bit of haste, staring down at her glazed digit in awe. "And I made my best friend have an orgasm…" she says, shaking her head with a grin.

I giggle. "What a day, right?"

"Indeed… So, what exactly happened after this thing swelled inside of you? Like, how long did it take before you could start feeling what it felt?"

I hop off the counter then, on our way to the living room, I start telling her about the minutes leading up to the tingling and burning. By the time we sit side by side on the couch, I'm just getting to the part about me soaking in the river. After that, I touch on the painful cramps and go into graphic detail about how my yoni flower expelled pink and white chunks, going as far as showing her the video I took in the middle of the night.

"And then, when I woke up," I say, "I didn't feel stuffed anymore even though it was still there. And when I tried to pull it out—"

"You realized you could feel every part of it you touched…"

"Mm-hm…"

"How are you not freaking out about this?"

I shrug. "Because I love plants and I feel like I've unified with one in the best way, even though I'm not so sure anymore that this is a plant anymore…"

"Honestly? I don't think it is either."

"Does my mycologist bestie think that this is a fungus?"

Priya nods. "It's got to be, right? You're a botanist, so how many plants have you heard of that can grow on or in vertebrates or invertebrates? And how many have nerves?"

"Exactly zero for both conditions… But, when I first saw it, it looked so much like an Amorphophallus bulbifer wearing an inverted Stapelia schinzii as a skirt. And it smelled so sweet, like a pitcher plant that evolved to attract flies."

"Yeah… But there are sweet-smelling mushrooms. The candy cap mushroom, for instance, smells like maple syrup mixed with butterscotch. And some fungi look like flowers. Have you ever seen the starfish fungus named Aseroe rubra?"

I shake my head.

"Hold on." She taps away at her iPhone's screen then pulls up a picture of a mushroom with a light pink stalk and a cap that looks like a six-armed starfish whose exterior is lined with red, wrinkled skin. In the center of the star-shaped cap, there's brown gunk.

"It sort of looks like the flower between my leg," I whisper.

"Yeah, and let me show you a picture of one that doesn't have gleba—the uh… brown slime in the middle." She pulls up a picture from Wikipedia showing a starfish stinkhorn with a fleshy hole that leads to a hollow white stalk. "I mean, it not *exactly* like your situation since your yoni flower does smell like a sweet flower, whereas this stinkhorn smells of rotting meat. Also, the veins of your yoni flower's petals do resemble the vascular system on most plant leaves, and I really can't think of any fungi that have veins like a plant or a human… It's almost like… it's almost like a starfish fungus merged with Stapelia and an Amorphophallus…"

"Maybe that's it. Maybe it's a hybrid species of some kind."

"Unless its fungus that assimilates and fuses with whatever lifeform it comes in contact with…"

"A fungus that could fuse with a plant? Believable. A fungus that could fuse with an animal? Also believable. But for one to merge with both? How could nature produce such a thing? And, if it could, why aren't there more of them across the world?"

Priya nods. "Exactly. Which means that this thing is either just very plantlike fungus that needs to live out part of its life in a woman's yoni or it's a fungoid plant that needs the same thing."

"That's why I need Julie to use her access to the genetics lab to figure out exactly what this is while you take some samples to your job's mushroom lab to do what you do best."

"If it's some kind of Mycorrhizal fungi, I might be able to get it to germinate on a substrate blend of oak hardwood, sawdust, wheat brand, rice flour, vermiculite, seed meal, and water…" She taps her finger against her lips. "Do you have anything I can collect samples with now?"

I twist my mouth to the side. "I've got some sterile plastic bags I've been using for storing the dried fruits I sell at the farmer's market. Maybe we can flame sterilize a knife and gently scrape some cells off?"

Priya winces. "We can try…"

Once everything is gathered up, Priya passes one of my sharpest folding survival knives over the flame of a lighter to sterilize it.

"You ready?" she asks with an arched brow.

With a nod, I lift my feet onto the couch cushion then bring my knees to my chest and spread my legs. "Ready."

"Okay…" Holding the top left petal by my thigh with one hand, she lightly drags the knife across the leathery beige skin. "Does that hurt?" she asks after the scrapping sensation makes the petal flex in her hand.

"Nope, whatever you were just doing was perfect. Just feels like you're shaving my labia."

She resumes scraping until she gets a decent amount of the flower's cells on the knife's edge. "Alrighty, that should be good enough for me to test," she says, scrapping the sample into the baggy with another sterile knife. "And now for Julie's sample…"

Just as Priya finishes the second round of light scraping, the door opens and in walks the fair-skinned, redhead, Julie Bloom.

"Sorry I'm late, I just—" she freezes and stares at Priya kneeling between my spread legs. "Umm… ladies? What did I just walk in on?" When Priya looks over her shoulder with the knife inside the second baggy, Julie's emerald eyes widen. "And what's up with the knife?"

"You're going to want to sit down for this…" Priya says, scraping off the sample into the bag before standing up to block her view while I pull down my dress.

"I'm scared…" Julie groans.

"Don't be," I say calmly. "Everything is fine. But what you're about to see will absolutely freak you the fuck out…"

Julie freezes, blinking rapidly like there's dust in her eyes.

Priya gestures to the couch cushion beside me. "Seriously, have a seat."

Julie sits down hesitantly. "Okay… The suspense is killing me. Please show me."

"Just know that it's worse than it looks but I'm fine," I say.

Her eyes widen. "Dear *gawd*… Okay…"

Shifting to face her, I spread my legs wide then quickly lift my skirt. "RAWR!" I growl at the same time that I make my yoni flower bloom with a Kegel.

Julie's eyes go wide. "AHHHHH!" she screams, scrambling back and falling off of the couch.

Priya and I laugh hysterically.

"Why did you do that to her?" Priya says, still cracking up.

I'm laughing so hard, I'm crying. "I'm so sorry! I just couldn't help it!" I say, wiping away a tear.

"What the fuck was that thing?" Julie asks, trembling with her purse clutched to her breasts while the still laughing Priya tries to help our petrified friend up. "Some prank prop?"

Me and Priya shake our heads slowly, almost in sync.

"It's not a prank," I say, "but part of me wishes it was… Come back up on the couch and let me fill you in."

CHAPTER 8
THROUGH THE LOOKING-GLASS

Thursday, June 2

Normally, I enjoy being at work. Because how can a botanist who's been using weed to curb her anxiety for years not enjoy working with one of the most amazing plants in the world? Not only am I a well-paid Cannabis tester, but I'm also a researcher, a consultant for weed vendors, and a soil specialist—so my career is essentially my hobby, and I love every minute of it. But not this week. This week, I've been distracted, counting down the hours until my appointment with my OB/GYN today at noon while obsessively trying to come up with scenarios of what was happening inside of me every time my cervix spasmed and dilated, or every time I felt a tickle inside of my uterus. And then yesterday, it occurred to me that I've been peeing way less than normal despite drinking a gallon of water.

I'm not peeing because I'm dehydrated from consuming so much sugar these last few days to curb my unyielding sweet tooth. That's what I told myself, but I know that's not it. It's the flower. And I've been freaking out these last few days because that means, if it's affecting my bladder, this plant-fungus-yoni-thing isn't just contained to my vagina and uterus after all…

It's spreading to other organs and I don't know how much of my body it's going to mutate…

"Why don't you just go to the ER?" Julie asked when I updated her and Priya last night about how I'm peeing low volume trickles twice a day now.

"Because, other than the peeing issue and uterine tingling, I feel great. No cramps. No other weird pains. I'm not losing weight. That and I'm scared that if I see a doctor I don't trust, they're going to put me under, excise my affected vaginal flesh, and give me a hysterectomy to stop it from spreading," I replied.

"They can't do that without your consent…" Priya reasoned.

"Yeah, you're right," I said, staring off in the distance. *"But they might have me flown out to the CDC to be contained and studied. I need a doctor I can trust, so it's Dr. Sloane or no one at all. Because if this thing is going to kill me, there's nothing anyone can do, so I'd rather not spend my last days in a research lab or some shit."*

Even if any of that wasn't the case, ever since I first went to Dr. Sloane after I got vaginosis from masturbating with a soil-covered carrot from my garden—and after the time I got bits of leaves stuck way up between the crease around my cervix—she is the one person I trust with all the mishaps that happen from me sticking vegetation up my cooter. She is understanding and non-judgmental, and she's basically a good friend to me. If there's any doctor to see about this, it has to be her.

So why did I have to wait three days to see Dr. Sloane Quinn instead of going the day after returning from Hoh Rainforest? Well, because the one time I urgently needed to see her, she happened to be on vacation in Hawaii with her sister Mackenzie. I was told she would be back in town yesterday, but when I asked for an appointment today, her receptionist said Sloane's Thursday was booked solid. Thankfully, when I texted her this morning, my thoughtful doctor said she'd squeeze me in during her lunch break.

Of course, it's raining by the time I walk out of the Canna Farms office, so I pull my rain jacket's hood and hurry across the lot to my blue Honda Civic.

Even with the torrential downpour, I still make it from Tacoma to Julie's apartment in Seattle in thirty minutes flat. And, right as I pull into the spot beside her RAV4, she comes running out of her building towards me.

"Hey!" she says as she climbs into the passenger seat, shaking the water off of her umbrella.

"Hey, Julie!" I say with a bright smile. "Thanks so much for going to this appointment with me."

"Girl, you don't have to thank me! How are you today?"

"Anxious to find out what's going on inside me, but good otherwise. You know, aside from only peeing five drips of urine all day." A nervous laugh escapes me. "How're the genetic tests going?"

"Still trying to find conclusive genetic matches among known species flora and fungi, but it does seem to have sequences that match human, female DNA. That could just be from DNA it acquired from you. Though, I also found cells with a Y chromosome. And Catie was able to identify some protein markers that are similar to what's found in the cell walls mycorrhiza fungi..." Catie Holden is her friend and lab partner from her grad school research group, a girl who's partied with us three few times since Julie began grad school.

"So, it is a fungus?"

Julie shrugs. "I don't know, because there were traces of the genetic sequences from plant cell walls too, which supports what you observed when you looked at a sample the other day..."

On Monday as soon as I got to work, I went to the bathroom, scrapped a sample from my petal the way Priya did, plated it on a microscope slide with a drop of sterile DI water, and took it to the lab. What I saw was unlike any cell I've ever seen. It had a nucleus, but the other organelles were bizarre, and so was the cell wall...

"Damn it..." I grumble. "So still inconclusive..."

"Yup. Priya having any luck?" Julie asks.

"About the same as us. She can't get the samples to germinate in their usual wood, soil, and wheat substrate blend."

Julie reaches over and gives my shoulder a rub. "Don't worry, the three of us will figure this out before you know it."

I force a smile. "Without a doubt!"

But what if I don't have time…

With my hospital gown on, I climb up on the table and place my feet in the stirrups. Julie sits in the chair beside me and holds my hand.

Dr. Sloane turns around from where she's been setting up the equipment, and the second she looks between my legs, her eyes go wide and her jaw goes slack. "Oh… what the…" her words trail off. "You weren't exaggerating when you said a flower was growing out of your vagina… I seriously thought you meant your labia had spontaneously grown abnormally long or something…"

"If only that were the case…" I say with a sigh.

After I'm done catching her up to speed on how this yoni flower ended up merged to my vagina and what's been happening since, she hooks up the long, thin and flexible wire camera called a hysteroscope to the laptop, then she pushes the wormlike camera into my Yoni hole. Being penetrated by the fiberoptic cable feels so delicious that it makes my petals flex into a wide blossom.

"Does that hurt or does it feel uncomfortable?" she asks.

"Nope, it just feels like you're feeding a smooth Twizzler into me." I snicker.

"What a colorful description," she smirks.

On-screen, we watch as the LED lit camera pushes into a sap glazed tunnel of vibrant, salmon-pink flesh lined with ribbed, velvety folds.

"These rugae… it looks just like a vagina in here…" Sloane says in awe.

"It really does…" I whisper, my eyes widening when something too horrific to be a cervix comes into view.

What should look like a fleshy, pink donut with a tiny pinhole in the middle is now covered in a beige, leathery-looking skin that looks like chunky, coagulated oatmeal—flesh that resembles the pod-rind that I uncovered beneath the yoni flower. And the hole in the center isn't a pinhole at all, it's extremely dilated to the width of a quarter.

Sloane gulps hard. "I'm not sure what I'm looking at here…" she whispers "This off-white tissue that's grown over your cervix… I've never seen anything like it… It's too symmetrical to be cancerous, but it doesn't look like mammalian tissue either…" She feeds the camera an inch into the dilated hole and the light doesn't illuminate a two-inch-wide tunnel to my uterus, it instead reveals a strange membrane of puckered white flesh.

"What… What is that?" Julie whispers.

"It looks like… it looks like an albino butthole…" I say quietly.

Dr. Sloane nods. "You're not wrong, Allie… We're about an inch into your cervix and there's a sphincter where there shouldn't be one—you know, because the cervix isn't a sphincter, and there definitely shouldn't be a flap of skin inside the cervix…"

"So, it didn't just change my vagina…" I mutter.

"Let me see if I can get past this membrane," Sloan says, feeding the flexible camera's tube deeper into me. "Let me know if this hurts."

"Okay."

The second the scope pokes the center of the tight ring of *muscle*, it feels exactly like it does when something pokes my asshole, but better. And when it finally pushes through the tight ring of muscle, my petals throb just as this clear, amber liquid gushes out of the sphincter like syrup.

"Did that hurt?" Sloane asks.

It feels kind of good… But I don't want to tell her that. "It doesn't hurt, it's just uncomfortable. You can keep going."

"Look at that…" she says. "There's a pool of clear yellow liquid in your uterus…. It looks like your womb is covered in the same off-white-beige skin all the way through… And…" She angles the camera downward. "Are those *vines*… or roots?"

Four clear, white vines are strewn in a snakelike pattern across the walls of my uterus—if I can even call this a uterus anymore. One of the transparent rootlike structures zigzags up the posterior wall of white flesh, and another goes up the anterior wall. The other two go up into either fallopian tube. All of them have thin branches coming out of them, webbing my uterus like veins. There's symmetry, like it had to grow in certain locations…

"Wait, go back!" I blurt out.

"Which way?" Sloane asks.

"Up toward my belly."

"What…" she gasps when she sees the pear-shaped mass of white lumpy flesh. "It appears to be some sort of organ maybe?"

"It looks like the yellow sap is dripping from that little hole in the bottom of the mass…" I mutter, pointing at the snot-like string dangling from the pinhole just as it suddenly snaps shut. "Maybe this is where it stores sap?"

"Perhaps…" Sloan says. "And look at this…" She centers the camera on the throbbing root that goes from the top of the *uterus* into the flesh above the pear-shaped sap organ. "You said you haven't been urinating much lately, right?"

"Yeah, despite drinking near a gallon per day…"

"Well, you see that vein-root-looking thing right there," Sloane says, pointing at the screen. "That's about where the uterus touches the bladder… If it has modified your vagina and uterus this much, it's possible that it could have made alterations to other nearby organs if there's something it needs from your body."

"The only thing a fungus or a plant would need from a bladder is urea, and whatever excess minerals we urinate…" I mutter.

Dr. Sloane and Julie nod.

Sloane begins slowly reeling the endoscope cable out of me, and damn does it feel good. "We should probably get you an MRI…"

I'm stuck in the noisy MRI for twenty long minutes. And when Sloane lets me out, I change back into my clothes before we return to her office to interpret the scans.

"Look at that," Sloan says pointing at the side view cross-section. "Normally there should be a thin strip longitudinally between your bladder and uterus, denoting an empty space, but you have these narrow strips of dark horizontal lines. My guess? It's a tube that connects your uterus to your bladder, as I've suspected…" With her laser, she points at something dark in the middle. "And that dark spot at the center of the connecting tube could be a tiny sphincter that opens when it needs to pull in urine, which explains why your uterus isn't flooded with urine. That or it could be a filter." She shrugs. "And it's probably a filter since what leaked out of your *yoni* flower, as you call it, was sweet-smelling and viscous, like the lubricative sap that erupted out of the original flower in the video you showed me."

"Yeah… And what are these circular things in my fallopian tubes?" I ask, pointing at the dozens of ball-shaped objects in the scans of the front view.

"I was about to go over to that next," Sloane says, pausing to ponder the image. "Before I touch on the round objects, I'd like to point out that your fallopian tubes are much wider than they should be. I'd say they're almost 1.5 cm in diameter when they should be 1-4 mm."

"Which means that this yoni flower not only expanded my cervix but also my fallopian tubes…"

"I'm afraid so," Sloane says, twisting her mouth to the side. "That brings me to these round blobs… They are too large to be your unfertilized eggs. Unless you're pregnant with a dozen embryos the size of small gumballs, and those fertilized eggs failed to implant in the uterus…"

"So, what are they?" Julie pipes up.

"Well," Sloane begins, "if this *yoni flower* that's bonded to you *is* a plant: it could be fruits or seeds? But if it's a fungus… it might be some kind of spore cluster or fruiting body?" She turns from the scans to me.

"Okay then… So, be real with me, Sloane… Do you think this plant is going to spread any further and take over my organs until it kills me?"

Sloane curls her lips into her mouth. "Allie, I honestly can't say… Only time is going to tell how far this thing will spread. *If* it will spread anymore. Based on how bonded to you it is, and considering how healthy your vitals are, if I had to guess, I'd say that you're not in any *immediate* danger. You said that the cramping and tingling haven't happened since Monday, right?"

"Mm-hm," I hum.

"Okay, so since the rest of your MRI looks normal and free of this dark tissue here," she says, pointing at the dark parts of the scans lining my vagina and womb, "we can assume it has stopped spreading. Whether it's a fungus or a plant, this yoni flower seems to be in its preferred part of your body. So, unless it's in some sort of hibernative state before it undergoes another expansive transformation, I think the rest of your organs are safe. However, there's no telling if this organism is going to parasitize you to the point where it robs you of nutrients, so you're going to have to come in for regular bloodwork and checkups over the next few months until we're sure your health is not at risk."

I sigh. "Yeah… Okay…"

Sloane nods. "I know this probably goes without saying, but… with all of the alterations this organism has made to your reproductive organs, it is highly unlikely that you will ever be able to have children…"

Even though I had already come to that conclusion the second she put the hysteroscope into my horrifically mutated womb, my eyes burn and well with tears. "I thought that'd be the case…" I whimper with a sniffle, wiping the tears from my cheek.

"Allie, I'm so sorry," Julie says, hugging me tightly.

I sniffle again, squeezing her. "It's okay…" I snort hard. "At least I'm not dying. Yet. And if I want kids, I can always adopt…"

"Yeah…" Julie says, sweeping her hand up and down my back. "And don't say dying *yet*. You're not going to die. You're just not, okay?"

"Okay," I whimper.

"Stay strong, Allie," Sloane chimes in. "While I can't promise or guarantee anything, I'm fairly confident you can still have a long life ahead with the right treatment, should you ever need any."

"I trust you, Slone," I say as I separate from Julie's embrace. When Sloane hands me some tissues, I dab my eyes before blowing my nose. "Well, I guess that's it then…" I say, sanitizing my hands.

"You have my personal number, so call me whenever you need me," Sloane says to me. "I don't make it a practice to go out of my way for patients like this, but this is a special case and, since I am the only person that you'll trust with this, I will be your point medical care professional, okay?"

I nod. "Thank you so much! You don't know how much I appreciate that!" I extend my hand to her.

Sloane offers me a hug instead, so we embrace.

"Alright," I sigh. "I won't take any more of your time."

"Okie-dokie. See you next Friday?"

I nod. "Next Friday works! Bye, Sloane!"

"See you, Allie! Take care!"

Julie wraps her arm around me as we step into the hallway. "You alright, Allie?"

I huff. "I guess so. I could really use a drink or ten, though."

"I gotta run back to the lab for a bit, but if you want to get shit-faced tonight—"

"Evergreen Tavern's Thirsty Thursday happy hour starts at four," I blurt out.

"Get out of my head!" Julie says, shaking me by the shoulder. "Are you going back to work?"

"Hell no! Not after that…"

"Didn't think so. Unfortunately, my project requires my attention. But you've got the key to my place, so go curl up in my bed with some hot tea or wine. I should be back in a few hours."

I smile. "I like the sound of that!"

CHAPTER 9
PENIS/GUYTRAP

Thursday

The only times I ever really get blackout, dancing on tables, making out with random guys drunk are the nights following incredibly stressful days. Like that Friday before spring break this past April when I caught my boyfriend of two years cheating on me, after a grueling week of midterms no less.

Spending all week thinking I might die, seeing on camera that my uterus looks like an alien insect pod, getting confirmation that I'll probably never have children all because I just had to screw a phallus growing out of the ground—all of that is why it's only 10:30 P.M. and I'm already losing time from blacking in and out.

I remember drinking a bottle of wine at Julie's, going to Evergreen Tavern, taking shots, chatting up some guys who bought us drinks, then… Boom, I'm dancing like a maniac one minute, then the next minute I'm stumbling into the lobby of an apartment building with some random hot guy who I barely remember meeting.

The second that me and the guy whose name may or may not be Matty step into his apartment's elevator, I mash my lips into his with desperation and shove my tongue into his mouth. Our make-out session is sloppy as all hell, but he doesn't seem to mind by the way he's trying to make me gag by tonguing my tonsils.

When he starts caressing me from my back to my ass, my yoni flower throbs into a blossom, gushing sap as my petals press hard against my thighs. That's a reminder that I have to do everything in my power to keep this guy from seeing the horror between my legs.

Suddenly, his hand finds its way on my inner thigh and he slowly caresses his way up to my sap dripping petals. The elevator dings the moment I grab his hand. *As bad as I want him to finger me, I'd rather not have him freak out before I get some much-needed dick.*

"I'm gonna make you wait a little bit longer, Matty," I slur, holding his hand and leading him out of the elevator.

"Allie," he says in a raspy growl. He pulls me in and plants a hungry kiss on my lips. "I know you're going to be worth every second of this wait."

We make out as we make our way down the hall, me walking backward and giving his long carrot of a cock an over-the-pants rubbing while he steers me to his apartment. After my back slams into the apartment door and I hear those keys jingle, I know it's finally almost time to get my flower fucked.

Ever since I started sensing what the yoni flower felt, I've been imagining what'd it'd be like to get dicked-down. And while I've masturbated my floral starfish's tight hole every night before bed with an asparagus and a carrot, I know it's going to be way better to have an actual man rail me now that my hole is two times more sensitive than it was before merging with the yoni flower. The anticipation of getting plowed by a sexy stranger sends excitement and arousal coursing through me, making my chest heave—making my petals blossom so hard they splash warm sap from my drooling hole onto my thighs. And as he backs me into the apartment, I peek over his shoulder and spot the trail of glistening syrup I left in the hallway.

As he's shutting the door, I drop my purse by the coat rack. With both of us panting and smacking lips, he steers me back to his room. The moment we stumble through the doorway, he reaches over and flicks on the switch for a lamp in the corner by the bed that bathes the room in a warm, amber light.

"If you don't mind, I'd like it if we kept it dark, okay?"

Matty eyes me curiously. "Aw, come on. I want to see your beautiful body, Allie."

"I'm just really shy. Please?"

"Whatever makes you comfortable, gorgeous." He reaches back and flips the switch down, plunging the room back into darkness with only a few bands of dull, yellow light from the streetlamps providing just enough illumination to outline our forms. He then takes me by the hands and starts walking backwards toward the bed.

His lips find mine again and his kiss dizzies me, robbing me of my breath. When he bumps into the bed, I unbuckle his jeans while he pulls his shirt off. I yank down his pants and boxers in one go.

"Get in bed. I want to ride you." I whisper in a sultry slur.

The silhouette of his head nods. "You sure you don't want me to take care of you first? I don't mind going down on you because I know you taste as sweet and delicious as you smell." He pecks my lips and his tongue flicks mine as he squeezes my ass.

You have no idea… "Maybe later. Right now, I want to ride you into oblivion."

"Fuck… If that's what you want, I won't argue," he whispers, sitting on the edge of the bed and crawling back to the headboard.

"You don't need a condom," I whisper when I see him reaching for his nightstand. "I can't have kids, so I want you to feel me. I want you to feel how wet I am for you."

The silhouette of his head nods eagerly.

I quickly kick off my shoes. With my dress still on, I crawl across the bed, focusing as hard as I can to keep my pussy petals splayed out nice and wide so he doesn't feel them dragging across his skin as I straddle him. When his rock-hard cock slides across a petal and pokes my flower's slit, I moan hard.

"Fucking hell… You are so wet! Damn, I feel you dripping on my cock!" he grunts.

"That's what you do to me, Matty," I say, curling my fingers around his sap-lubed dick and giving him a few strokes.

"That's what you do to me," he groans. "I've been rock-hard since the second I walked up to you—AHHH!" he roars as I lower myself on him, engulfing the head of his cock with my flower's tight opening. "Oh… yeah… Wow!" he says as my yoni hole swallows half of his cock. "Ugh… yeah… You're so fucking wet and soft! And so incredibly fucking tight!" He growls. "How? How are you this tight and wet?" His words come out strained. His body spasms as I slam down on his dong, taking him as far as he can go.

"I'm gifted," I whisper, moaning as I slowly rise from his cock.

There are two things I've learned to do over the last three days. One is how to move each petal individually. The other is how to close my petals into the shape of an empty banana peel, sort of like a firm bird beak made of five flat muscles. What I've been doing is closing it into the cone shape around whatever veggie toy I'm playing with that night, then I fuck the petals as though my pussy has become an external tube hanging out of my body. Then I push the cucumber or whatever I'm using into it, splaying my clenched petals as its girth pushes toward the yoni hole. It feels fan-fucking-tastic.

I wonder if I can do my petal-job-technique while drunk…

It takes a bit of focus, but when the head of his cock is about to leave my flower's hole, I concentrate on wrapping my pussy petals around his shaft like I'm unpeeling a banana in reverse, using my meat leaves like fingers to squeeze his dick with the perfect amount of pressure. Essentially, I'm giving him a blowjob but using my pussy petals as lips—a petal job, or PJ as I call it.

"Oh shit!" he groans, his body quaking so hard that the bed frame rattles. "What are you doing? That feels fucking amazing!"

I moan as his dick glides against my slippery petals toward their tips. "This is why I wanted to take care of you. Because I know how to please a man better than anyone."

"Yes, you fucking do, baby!" he says with a strained voice. His entire body spasms even harder as I lower myself onto him, his cock splaying my petals until he splits them apart and plunges back into my tight hole with a loud spurting, squelch of a sound. "Oof… Keep this up and I won't last long, sweetheart."

Seconds after I pick up the pace, I start panting heavily. "I'm getting close to coming too—ahhh!" I cry out.

I bounce on his dick, harder and faster every few rounds, my tightness gushing and spurting sap with every descent, squelching with each rise. As I ride him, my core jumps from a strange sensation in my womb that feels like something is moving from where I imagine my fallopian tubes are.

Oh no… what's happening now?

As that thought leaves my mind, as I slam down on him hard and impale myself with his cock as deep as it'll go, an unexpected climax explodes in the depths of my yoni flower, triggering a powerful wave of rhythmic contractions through my uterus. It's more intense and incredible than anything I've ever felt before.

"Allie…" he groans. "I'm—GARR-GAHHH!" he roars like a feral beast as his cock throbs in my clenching hole, spurting his liquid warmth deep into me.

Suddenly, my *pussy* stops contracting and just cramps hard, clamping around his meat rod like a fist trying to squeeze every last drop out of juice from a lime. At that exact moment, my petals curl around his crotch like it's trying to eat his manhood.

"Oh! Ow! Allie!"

"Ah!" I cry out too from the powerful cramp. "Sorry! I don't know what's happening, I'm cramping up! Just—just give me a sec!"

No matter what I do, I can't get my petals or my yoni's canal to relax. And even though my yoni muscles have locked up, my uterus is pulsating like a giant heart.

Matty writhes and groans beneath me. "Ow! Holy shit you're crushing my dick!"

"Sorry! Sorry! I'm trying to make it stop! Just don't move!"

"Sweet baby Jesus!" he growls, writhing beneath me.

That's when I feel it. Something the size and shape of a gumball is bulging down through my cervix.

Not a gumball… A seed… or a fungal egg… Whatever I saw on the MRI today…

Rhythmic contractions force the seed-egg thing through where I imagine my new cervical sphincter is. Peristalsis-like contractions then slowly force the ball down into my modified birth canal. I feel it bulging down right to where the head of his cock is. My yoni canal suddenly relaxes only to clench even harder around him a split-second later. Over and over, that happens until it feels like a grape has just popped between my cervix and his cockhead, spilling something thick between us.

"Allie!" he groans, squirming beneath me. "Has this ever happened before?"

"Never! Just, don't say anything, I'm trying to relax and you're stressing me out."

Of all four times that I've masturbated my yoni hole to orgasm with carrots, asparagus, and cucumbers, never have I once cramped in the middle of it.

I cramped the second after he came in me… Does semen make this flower behave this way?

We lay with our genitals conjoined for maybe two long minutes with the top half of my Yoni canal contracting while the bottom half remains gripped around him like a Superman's fist.

Then, out of nowhere, my petals and my *pussy* relax. Now I move fast, pulling his still hard cock out during my scramble of a dismount.

"Ooof," Matty huffs as he sits up.

"Sheesh!" I blow out, pulling the skirt down before swinging my legs over the edge of the bed. "I. Am. So. Sorry. Matty! That *literally* has never happened to me before."

"I guess I just made you cum that hard, didn't I?" He chuckles as he leans over and clicks on the lamp on the end table.

Now that the room is illuminated, I look between my legs, staring in confusion at the thick white gunk dripping down the inside of my bottom petals.

"What the…" I hear Matty say.

When I look back, I find him just staring down at his dick. My eyes widen when I realize that the head of his penis and the first two inches of his manhood is smeared with something like thick, sticky cookie dough or cottage cheese. As we're both staring in silence, he pinches something on his tip then peels off what looks like a piece of white latex glove from the head of his cream-covered cock, slimy strings stretching between the flappy material and his member like fresh gum that just got stepped on.

Is that what I felt pop in me? Did… did the seed-egg or whatever rupture on his cock… My heart starts racing. *Oh no… Oh no…*

"You came hard around me you made my cum all frothy or some shit…" He laughs nervously as he tries wiping the stuff off.

"Or maybe it's just discharge?" I wince.

"Maybe…" After vigorously rubbing his deflating cock, he pulls his thumb away and stringy gunk stretches between the digit and his slime-covered glans. "Whatever this shit is, I can't wipe it off!"

"Just, like, try soap and water or something."

"Yeah… I gotta piss anyway," he says, swinging his legs over the bed and rising, still looking down at his cock while trying to rub the stuff off.

As soon as he shuts the bathroom door, I spring out of bed. "What was I thinking?" I whisper, tiptoeing across the room and gathering my scattered shoes.

You knew damn well that you shouldn't be letting a guy fuck you raw when you didn't know what this yoni flower would do to a penis…

Even drunk I knew this was a bad idea, but I was in a 'You only live once' mood and I desperately needed some loving. Because there's still part of me worried that I might die, and I want to enjoy life as much as I can before anything worse happens.

"Yo, this shit still isn't coming off, *and* I'm using a washcloth!" Matty shouts from the bathroom as I'm picking up my purse.

I picture the batter smeared all over the top of his dick. I imagine it not coming off because it's actually the mycelium of a fungus that's rapidly threading into his flesh like a mushroom growing into a tree trunk.

What have I done?

"I'm really fucking embarrassed so I'm just going to go!" I shout, running out of his apartment barefoot before he even has a chance to respond.

I imagine the cottage cheese-like gunk mutating his cock the way that this flower did to my vagina.

"What the fuck did you do, Allie?" I whisper to myself, repeatedly smashing the elevator button.

When I hear a door down the hall open, I don't look back to see if it's Matty, I just sprint down the hall and burst through the door into the stairwell. And when I get two flights down, I slump against the wall of the landing and collapse to the floor. Curious as to see if the creamy gunk is stuck to my petals the way it was to his cock, I hike up my skirt, spread my legs, and make my flower blossom while pulling the top petal to my belly so I can see. I watch as what looks like beads of milk roll down the fleshy, pink underside of the bottom left petal.

Whatever is running out of me is way waterier than what's plastered on Matty's dick… It looks like the yoni flower is secreting something to clean itself out the way a vagina would… I guess it makes sense that whatever this stuff is wouldn't stick to the flower.

After closing my legs and readjusting my skirt, I pull out my phone, trembling as I struggle to navigate to my Uber app. I'm shuddering because I can't stop thinking about all the horrible things that might happen to my one-night-stand's reproductive organs if what's now stuck to his flesh corrupts him the way this plant did to me.

Matty… I'm so sorry…

"God," I say, slapping my palm against my forehead, "I really hope nothing bad happens to him…"

CHAPTER 10
FRUITING BODY

Friday

Ten minutes after picking me up, the Uber driver drops me off at Julie's apartment complex. Halfway down the path to her building's entrance, my womb contracts rhythmically out of nowhere. It's not the painful kind I woke up to that night in my tent, it's pleasant, like the uterine orgasm I felt after riding Matty to climax. It feels so good, I moan as my knees go weak and buckle beneath me. Being as drunk as I am, I lose my balance and swerve off the pavement into the grass, tripping over a sprinkler system. At that same moment, I swear I feel another grape-sized bulge popping out of my yoni hole, but when I look at the grass beneath me, I don't see any weird egg-things laying in the grass.

I'm probably just imagining things, I think, stepping back onto the pavement.

As soon as I stumble into her apartment, I hear Julie snoring like a bear the way she tends to do when she's drunk. When I peek into the room at her, a hazy memory pops into my head. *"It might not be a good idea to fuck anyone until we know what we're dealing with."* That's what she told me when she saw me getting all flirty with Matty before I left.

"Fuck that! It's not like this yoni flower is going to clamp onto some guy's dick and leave me for him or something," is what I slurred back.

It didn't leave me for Matty, but it did leave something stuck to him…

Despite how badly I want to wake her up so I can vent, I shut her bedroom door softly then I lie down on the couch. This isn't a story I feel like telling twice, so I'm just going to wait until the girls are both together at my house tomorrow morning before our road trip to Hoh Rainforest—before our expedition to investigate the pod so we can find out what lies beneath it and also acquire some genetic material straight from the source.

Normally, I'd pass out as soon as I lay down after drinking as much as I did tonight, but here I am curled up on the couch, too traumatized by what happened with my one-night-stand to fall asleep. I lay there so long researching fungi on my phone that I sober up enough to drive.

Julie's place in Olympia is only 12 miles from my house, so it only takes me 24 minutes to pull up in my driveway. Just as I'm climbing out of my car, my womb begins contracting pleasantly again as it did earlier. Once again, the pleasure makes my knees buckle beneath me to the point that I have to plant a hand on my doorframe to steady myself. And, the second I unlock my door and step inside, I feel it.

"Oooof," I groan in pleasure as another gumball-sized object bulges its way down through my cervix's sphincter.

The muscles in my *pussy* contract, starting from near the cervix then rippling downwards to my yoni flower's opening. Each contraction makes me moan. Each contraction quickly pushes the bulge toward the exit. When it finally reaches my opening, there's a bubbly spurt, and then something thuds against the floor with a splat right before I reach the light switch.

Being careful not to crush it, I take a step to the side then flick the switch up.

"What the…" I whisper, staring down at this glistening, semi-translucent, off-white, gelatinous ball that's sitting in a slow-spreading puddle of my sap. "Maybe something did fall out of me outside of Julie's…"

Right as I'm squatting down to pick it up, my yoni spasms, spurting and bubbling as another ball bulges through my tight opening and bounces with another sticky splat.

"Holy shit, it feels like I'm laying tiny eggs," I whisper as I pick up the first ball-like mass.

Like the testicle-lychee-looking thing I found in the yoni's fruit sac, the membrane is a bit leathery. When I give it a gentle squeeze, it feels firm, but it squishes a little when I increase pressure. If I had to compare it to something, I'd say it's like squeezing a cherry. I can tell it won't take much pressure to make this thing pop.

To make sure there are no more inside of my cavity, I slip a finger into my yoni hole, pushing as deep as I can go. I don't find any, nor do I feel any of the leftover waxy batter that smeared all over Matty's dick. And when I pull my finger out, I'm relieved to find that it's only covered in the usual clear sap.

Now I pick up the second gelatinous ball and roll them both around in my palm like dice. *These things must be what my contractions popped against Matty's cock… Are they fruits? Seeds? A ball of spores?*

"Only one way to find out…" I think, heading to the kitchen.

Once I pull on a pair of latex gloves, I carefully pick up the smallest ball I've just birthed then I head down to the basement where I've been keeping the cardboard box containing the mushroom growing kit that Priya brought over on Tuesday. It's got peat moss, oak hardwood, sawdust, wheat brand, rice flour, vermiculite, and seed meal—everything a Mycorrhizal fungus needs to grow, all I have to do is add water, mix it, then add mycelium. So, if this yoni flower is actually a fungus, and if this ball *is* a cluster of spores or mycelium, something should grow.

A few cups of water are added to the substrate, then I give it a thorough mix inside the box. When I'm all finished, I place the gelatinous ball in the center of the earthy mix that looks like woodchip speckled soil, then I press my thumb down on it until it pops, gushing this thick, off-white cream that looks like cookie batter. There are no seeds in it. No part of this looks like a squished fruit.

I wonder if this goo is a mass of liquid spores…

"Gross," I groan as thick, sticky strings stretch between the popped ball's flat skin and my thumb like gum.

If they are liquid spores, does that mean that my womb is the fruiting body of this fungus? Or does that mean I am the fruiting body?

When I rub the gunk on my glove between my thumb and pointer, it quickly thickens and glues the two latex fingers of the glove together.

Sheesh… I guess that's exactly what it did to Matty's dick, I think, covering the exploded mass with a layer of the wet substrate. *It stuck to his flesh, but it didn't glue his flesh to the inside of my yoni… Because why would it? This flower wouldn't be able to spread any more of these ball-things if it blocked itself off, so it stands to reason that it secrets an enzyme or something to dissolve this gummy goop…*

After tossing the gloves and putting on a fresh pair, I grab the flashlight from the drawer before picking up the last yoni ball that I left sitting on a napkin by the sink. Now I head out through the back door and trek to the clearing in the woods where I buried the lychee-looking testicle thing. Just using my bare hands, I dig a six-inch hole a few feet away from where I planted the lychee-testicle-thing, then I drop in the gross, un-popped egg-ball that I birthed tonight, burying it intact to see if it makes a difference.

"Guess we'll see which one of these things will grow into a yoni flower," I say to myself, shining my flashlight around to illuminate the path through the woods.

Hopefully, it doesn't take too long. I need answers. ASAP.

CHAPTER 11
LINGA EPIMORPHOSIS

Friday

This far off the trail, there's barely any visible soil, just lush ferns, soft sprouts, and other greenery blanketing the Hoh Rainforest floor. Soft leaves brush my calves as I long-step over the hidden tree log that I tripped over six days ago. Once Priya and Julie are safely over the obstacle, I lead them through a cluster of big leaf maples and around a massive Sitka spruce before crawling under the bowed archway of a bent tree trunk that has long, dripping lichens dangling from it like wet hair.

"Allie?" Julie says panting semi-hard. Despite being a skinny-Minnie, she's not the type to exercise or do cardio of any kind. "How did you even know to go this way when you first wandered through here?"

"I *didn't* know," I say, caressing a mossy trunk as we weave through a thicket of trees. "I just looked at my compass and decided to travel north-ish." I pause as I push through a wall of dense foliage. "And then when I heard the trickle of this stream," I say, pointing to the narrow body of water that's barely visible through the pair of trees ahead, "I just decided to follow it. A few miles later, I smelled the yoni flower and just kept walking in the direction of the scent."

"How much further do we have?" Priya asks. "This industrial-size borescope is heavy as heck!" Inspired by having an endoscope exploring the inside of my yoni flower and my mutated womb, I decided to stop at Lowes on the way here to buy an industrial endoscope with a flexible, 16.4 ft long fiberscope so we can take a look inside the pod.

"Uh, we shouldn't be too far now," I respond. "Maybe another mile? Once we hear the waterfall, we'll only be a quarter mile from where I found the flower."

"Are you sure we're not lost?" Julie asks in a whiny voice. "We're, like, two miles off-trail and it feels like we're walking in a circle."

I point at the neon orange tape that I left dangling on the tree branch six days ago. "You see that? That's one of the breadcrumbs I left so I could make it back to the path. The next one should be coming up near a fallen tree in about a quarter-mile."

"Good, because it's getting close to evening and it'd suck to have to set up camp for the night just to pack up and do it again when we get to the yoni hollow."

She's right, it is getting late. Thanks to my hangover, we left much later than I wanted to—around 10:50 a.m. And after a three-hour drive from Olympia to the Olympic National Forest lot that I parked at last time, we probably won't reach the hollow in the clearing until near sunset, which means we'll barely have any time to set up camp, never mind have the time today to dig up that Yoni pod and collect samples…

Sure enough, just over a mile later, we follow the creek to the hidden waterfall where the rushing white water is spilling down the ten-foot-high, moss-covered rocks into the clear pond.

"This is gorgeous!" Priya says, climbing on top of the log bordering the pond to get a better view. "Magical!"

"Right?" I say, squatting down and splashing some cool water onto my face and my arms. "This was the surprise I told you about!"

"Um," Julie hums, squatting beside me, "we're coming back to swim here tomorrow morning before we get to work, right?"

"Does this water look deep enough to *swim* in, Julie?" Priya says with a smirk. "It's *maybe* knee-deep by the waterfall."

"Fine, we're coming back here to *sit* in the water tomorrow, right?" Julie asks me while splashing Priya.

Smiling, Priya gasps then splashes her back. As she tries to stand, she loses her balance on the log and falls into the pond. "Great..." she groans, whipping back her drenched hair.

"That's one way to beat this June heat," Julie mutters, giggling.

I cackle as I help her up. "To answer your question, yes. I planned on soaking in this pond tomorrow before we get to work, and after we're done digging up the pod because it's going to be hot as heck tomorrow. This is why I told you all to pack bikinis!"

"And here I thought you just meant we'd stop at the beach on the way back," Priya says, ringing out her shirt.

Following a short rest, I lead the girls through the path of mushy soil between the rocks and the wall of trees until the gigantic spruce with the hollow comes into view beyond the trees and underbrush.

"And there it is," I say, pushing through the foliage and stepping into the clearing where nothing grows. "That mound in the middle of the hollow? That's where my yoni flower came from..."

Priya strolls up beside me and looks up to the dead, towering tree in the center of the clearing. "Wow... this thing is gigantic," she says in awe.

"And this hollow is bigger than my freaking bedroom," Julie says, planting her hand on the bark as she peeks inside the trunk and looks around.

I brush past her as I step into the hollow, staring in confusion at the yoni stalk. It's no longer limp and shriveled like it was when I left it. Not only is it fully erect, but the top half of it is also now covered in what looks like hardened, lumpy, beige pudding.

It looks just like Matty's dick did last night…

And the tip of the stalk that popped out of the phallic spadix after it got stuck in me is no longer flat, it's sort of rounded and wider than the rest of the shaft, like it's regrowing its bulbous tip…

"Allie, didn't you say that the stalk shriveled up and went limp after the linga part of the plant got stuck in you…?" Priya says in awe.

"Hold on," Julie blurts out before I can answer, "what the heck is a linga?"

"It's the male counterpart to the yoni," she replies.

"Oh, it's a *dick*," Julie says with a smirk, turning to me. "Okay, so, it's in the skirted linga flower stage until it ends up fusing to someone's vagina, *then* it becomes a yoni flower?"

"You know what?" I say, nodding. "The linga flower stage is what we should call this form of the plant-fungus-thing." I turn to Priya. "And to answer your question, it wasn't like this when I left it…" I grab my phone and pull up the picture of the limp stalk. "Here, look."

Priya takes it from me. "Oh, wow. Yeah, it looked like it was dead in this picture."

"Guess that means it's regenerating a new linga for someone else to fuck," Julie adds, smirking at me. "What's it called again when an organism regrows a limb? Epimorphosis?"

"Yup," I say, reaching out and curling my fingers around the stalk. The base of it is leathery, smooth, and firm like I remember.

Whatever the lumpy stuff is that's covering the top half, it's soft, squishy, and a bit elastic when I pull it, like cheek skin. It's warm like it too—warmer than it was when it was a fully formed linga spadix...

It feels alive...

Priya squats to my left, handing the phone back to me. "Oh, wow," she says after cautiously caressing the plant's phallus. "It's, like, body temperature."

Julie squats to my right and curls her fingers around it after I pull my hand away. "Ooh, and it's squishy and stiff in the best way..." She turns to me and Priya. "Girls, let's try our best not to fuck this thing this weekend, okay?"

Smirking, I give her a gentle shove. "The aromatic aphrodisiac isn't in the air anymore so I don't think you two will have a problem with that."

"Maybe *you* don't smell it, but *we* do," Julie says, leaning over and sniffing over my skirt. "Did you forget you always smell like lust, cookies, and flowers? We're always a little horny around you..."

I look from her to Priya. "Wait, really?"

Both girls nod.

"Not gonna lie," Julie says, wince-smiling, "I had to leave the room a few times to masturbate while I was at your house..."

"We didn't want to say anything and make you feel uncomfortable," Priya replies, "but yeah. We both get a little turned on and damp down there whenever we're in the same room as you."

I bobble my head. "Oh wow... I mean, I had my suspicions that it didn't just wear off after the first day." I turn to Julie. "When we went out the other night, you were flirtier than I've ever seen you."

"Oh yeah… The alcohol made it more intense. But as soon as you left with what's-his-face, I came to my senses and decided not to go home with that Kevin guy I was sucking face with."

"You know… pheromones like that would sell…" I say, rising from my squat. "Maybe I should bottle my sap and sell it at the farmer's market along with my dried fruits." I laugh.

Priya giggles. "Somehow I feel like a substance dripping out of a mystery organism that's merged with your vajayjay wouldn't be FDA approved."

"Hey, they don't have to know where it came from," I say, swinging off my backpack. "Anyhoo, let's set up the tent and get a fire going before it gets too late."

CHAPTER 12
WHAT LIES BENEATH

Saturday

A loud bird squawking in the canopy above wakes us right around dawn. The temperature dropped to the low-50s last night and it's not supposed to get up into the low-70s until closer to noon, so we all decide to rest in our cozy, three-person tent for a few more hours until it warms up a bit.

Around 9:00, I awake again to Priya unzipping the tent.

"Sorry, gotta pee!" she whispers.

"You're fine," I groan, stretching as I sit up. "I'll get the fire going and work on breakfast."

"Yum, breakfast," Julie mutters sleepily from the sleeping bag beside me.

Last night, we set up the tent so that three-quarters of it is inside the tree's hollow with the entrance to it a few feet away from the regrowing linga flower. So, when I crawl out, I have to slink around the soil mound to get outside. To my surprise, it's actually sunny for once and it feels like it's in the mid-60s already. It's warm enough to take off my hoody and swap my sweatpants for my skirt, but I'll probably just wait until after we eat.

After breakfast, we change into our bikinis, grab our towels, then hike the quarter-mile down to the waterfall. Walking around with flower petals spilling out of my bikini bottoms is not only uncomfortable, but it also makes me feel like a fool. Like, if I wasn't wearing them, my petals would be visible anyway. And it's not like they haven't seen my yoni flower in all of its glory up-close and personal, so I could just take these bottoms off. Still, I choose not to.

This is the rest of my life now… I can never go to the beach or a pool again. Unless I wear a long swimming skirt or something…

Me and the girls end up relaxing and splashing around in the waterfall's shallow pool for almost two hours before heading back to camp. Since it's sunny and already about 73 °F now, we all just decide to keep our bikinis on. Except for me. I keep the top on, but I trade the bikini bottoms for a skirt since underwear is super uncomfortable for my sensitive petals.

While the girls start digging from the ends with shovels, I hand-scoop away the dirt around the base of the stalk. *Looks like the linga spadix isn't the only part regrowing,* I think, fondling the mushy, partially regenerated sac and the tiny balls inside.

It takes just under ten minutes for us to dig up the layer of soil covering the pod. After I shovel away the final patch of soil and dump it on the dirt pile, we all stand around staring down at this veiny, lumpy, glistening, cream-colored rind with disgust plastered on our sweaty faces.

Just like I thought, the pod is as long and wide as the soil bulge was.

"This thing is fucking gross…" Julie groans.

"Looks like a body bag made of tapioca pudding…" Priya says.

"Or like a sarcophagus made of week-old oatmeal," I groan.

"No, that's exactly what it looks like…" Priya whispers. "A sarcophagus… A sarcophagus made of mutated flesh…"

"Gawd, it smells like earthworms, rotting flowers, skunk, and something spoiled…" Julie adds.

I point at the stalk that's protruding from the lower half of the pod like a chrysalis with a boner. "Look how those tan veins snake up from the rind to the stalk…"

Priya squats before the pod then she presses down on it with two fingers. "This thing definitely has some kind of metabolism because it's even warmer than the stalk is…" She snatches her hand away like something inside just poked her.

"What should we do?" Julie says, turning to me. "Cut around the edges and peel it back like a yogurt lid?"

I shake my head. "Before we do *that*, maybe we should cut a small hole out and put the $60, industrial-sized endoscope to use so we can get an idea what we're dealing with first."

"Good idea," Julie says, nodding. "I'll grab it."

Like the scientists we are, we all put on safety glasses and gloves before doing anything. Kneeling at the *southern* end of the flesh sarcophagus where the *feet* would be in relation to the phallus and its ball sac, I stab the pod with my survival knife, plunging it into something that feels as thick and tough as steak. Right as the knife's guard mashes into the meaty rind, this sweet and pungent-smelling, brownish-yellow liquid oozes out around the blade.

"Bleh," I gag. *Why is it brown? What happened to the white gunk that oozed out when I pushed down on the pod?*

"Oh, that's nasty," Julie says, gagging as she runs away.

Slowly, I cut a six-inch diameter circle into the pod, leaving a little bit of the skin attached so I can peel it open like a flesh door before ripping it off, that way it doesn't fall inside. The circular chunk that I tear away is nearly two inches thick and squishy like a slab of raw steak. "You know what this looks like?" I say, examining it. "The kombucha SCOBY-pellicle-membrane-thing— the gelatinous microbial mat that floats at the top after fermentation…"

"You're right," Priya gags as she holds out the sample container for me to drop it in. "We should pipette some goo into the container and cover the sample with it so it doesn't dry out."

I nod. "Good thinking."

Julie hands me a disposable plastic pipette then I squeeze it before plunging it into the hole. When I pull out the slime-filled pipette, there are thick strings of mucus dripping off of it like snot, dripping all over the edge of the sample container. It takes, like, six squeezes of the bulb to empty all the viscousness on top of the pod slice. Now I repeat the process until it the sample is submerged.

"Care to do the honors, Priya?" Julie asks, extending the camera end of the endoscope's cable to her.

"Sure," she says, taking it. "This thing is waterproof, right?"

"Hell yeah, it is!" I say, scrunching up my face. "Now, is it yoni slime-proof? Who knows," I laugh as Julie hands me the 1080p LCD screen to me.

Using the controls on the handheld screen, I turn on the LED light to the brightest setting, then Priya feeds the cable into the hole, angling it toward the stalk. Through the murky amber liquid, two masses come into view on the underside of the pod ceiling right below where the stalk is. One mass is brownish and round. The other is a lumpy, white, pear-shaped mass that looks *exactly* like a larger version of the growth we saw in my womb. Also, both organs have these fleshy cords growing down out of them—veins that vanish into the murky depths of the pod.

"Are those… organs?" I say softly.

"Looks like it…" Priya says.

"Try poking the camera into that white organ," I say.

Priya does as instructed, ramming the cable into it. After the second poke, something clear and yellow gushes out from the stalk's bulbous tip.

"I think that's where the lubricative sap comes from..." I mutter. "Try poking the other one..."

She does, and a bit more yellow sap spurts out before this thick, white gunk oozes slowly from the stalk's tip.

"Um..." I say, touching it. After sniffing it, I rub the cream between my fingers. "I'm pretty sure this is the stuff the yoni flower jizzed into me—the thick goo that made the phallus swell and adhere to my skin..."

"Gross..." Julie says, scooping some of it up with her gloved finger and giving it a sniff. "Oof, that smells bitter..."

"Hmm..." Priya hums. "Since this brownish liquid you pipetted from the pod smells sweet, I wonder if this slime inside is a mass storage of sugars, proteins, and all of the other biochemical molecules this yoni flower needs. And maybe these organs use that to produce those two secretions for the phallus."

"There's only one way to find out," I say. "Julie, swab some gunk and sap samples."

"I'm on it!"

While Julie collects the pod's *ejaculate*, Priya feeds the camera downward. A few inches below the surface, we find a chaotic, interwoven net of cordlike structures. Some are fleshy, beige tubes that look like a web of thick earthworms. Those are interwoven with branched, ebony stems resembling a tangled mess of woody vines that have hooked protrusions. Some of those dark roots are growing into or out of the fleshy arteries.

"Those cords look like veins," I say softly, pointing at the wormlike tubes.

"And these dark brown, woody branched ones look like the rhizomorphs—the mycelium cords that the honey fungus mushroom uses to feed off of trees..." Priya tells us. "I bet these rhizomorphs aren't just in and on this pod, but it's likely growing out all over this area, drawing nutrients from surrounding plants and fungi, and delivering it back to this mass. That's how the Armillaria ostoyae mushrooms down in Malheur Nation Forest that I studied for my thesis operate—minus the nutrient storage pod, that is. The honey fungus covers 3.4 square miles and devours trees. If this pod has *this* much of a biomass underground, its roots might even extend beyond this clearing…"

"It looks like the fleshy veins are growing out of the rhizomorph cords and going up into the organs up top and the pod itself," I say.

"This is *too* freaky…" Julie whispers.

"It's unlike any plant or fungus I've ever seen…" Priya adds.

This horrific thing is what gave rise to the flower that ejaculated in me and subsequently fused to my flesh…

When Priya feeds the endoscope down maybe another foot into the pod, things start getting murkier from this thick layer of dark sludge about three feet down, so the floor of the pod isn't visible. All we can make out rising up through the net of fleshy and woody roots from the murkiness below are these erect, pale, cream-colored stalks that look like a mix between a giant white asparagus and the carnivorous sundew plant. Like asparagus, the tip is a rounded spear resembling a soft pinecone made of a tight cluster of round bract leaves—much like the top of a pinecone ginger, Zingiber zerumbet. As for the tubular stalk, the entire length of it is covered with these thick, black, hairlike structures that have little translucent, orange balls on the ends of them—just like tentacle leaves of the Drosera, or sundew.

"What the heck are those hairy asparagus things?" Julie asks.

"I don't know," I mutter. "But they're covered in the same sticky-looking hairs that sundew plants use to trap flies with before their leaves wrap around them like tentacles and digest them."

"Yeah, they do… But those ball-tipped hairs also look like the fruiting bodies of orange slime mold when you zoom in on them…"

"This thing…" I say in awe. "This thing has the warmth of a mammal, the flower, sap, and aroma of a plant, the capabilities of a fungus, phallus of a man's dick, the roots of a mushroom—"

"And the pod has the skin of a tapioca slime mold with the thickness and toughness of muscle tissue," Priya adds.

"Maybe it's some kind of ancient super organism," Julie mutters. "Like *the* protist that gave rise to the Plantae, Fungi, and Animalia kingdoms…"

"It's got to be something like that since you kept getting mixed DNA results," I say. "Either a protist or—"

"An *alien*…" Priya adds.

"I didn't want to say it," Julie whispers.

"I wonder how deep this thing goes," Priya says feeding the cable in.

"This endoscope is 16.5 feet," I say, "so just keep going until you hit the bottom then we can measure how much of the cable is coated in slime when we extract it."

"Good idea!"

The camera bumps into something another few feet past where the hairy white asparagus stalks stop being visible, meaning it's somewhere around three to four feet deep.

"Hey, before you pull it out, point it towards the ceiling and feed it towards the other end. I wanna see if there are any more organs along the top of the pod," I say.

"I'll see what I can do," Priya says.

When most of the slime-covered cable is out, Priya gets the camera over one of the fleshy tubes, using it as support so she can feed it horizontally.

"Hold on!" I blurt out. "What the heck is that?"

"What?" the girls say in unison, leaning against me to look at the screen.

"That!" I shout, pointing at this weird, skeletal-like structure that was hidden behind the sap and gunk organs. "It looks like…"

"Hip bones…" Julie gasps.

"No, they look *exactly* like the posterior side of the wing of ilium pelvis bones…" Priya adds as she pushes the camera closer.

I point at the base of the stalk that's right in the bottom center of what can only be a pelvis. "And the stalk is growing out exactly from the center of it, *exactly* where a dick would be if this was the pelvis of a man…"

Priya feeds the camera in further and, suspended from the pod rind's ceiling by transparent, fibrous tissue is what appears to be a ribcage with a spine running through the middle.

"Is there…" Julie gags. "Is there a fucking decomposed corpse inside of this fucking thing?" Suddenly, she springs up, sprints out of the tree hollow, then pukes.

"That's definitely a fucking skeleton…" I say as bile and acid rush up into my throat.

Both Priya and I get up at the same time and race out of the hollow. I wretch as she vomits her rehydrates eggs and bacon on the other side of the tree, then I puke right beside her.

"No wonder the dimensions of this mound are the size of a burial pit…" Priya groans, wiping her mouth. "This thing… it was a person…"

"Yeah…" I picture the lifelike phallus that I had *sex* with. "A person, specifically a *man*. Which means the dick-shaped fungus-plant or whatever the hell it is was that I fucked and let merged to my vagina was once an *actual* dick that this organism hijacked and incorporated into a part of its flowering-fruiting body or whatever…"

Julie wretches hard and I hear her vomit splash behind me. "That explains the human DNA I found that didn't match yours…" she mutters.

"But…" Priya says, dry heaving, "how could the spadix of the flower you masturbated with be his dick? About 2 inches of the stalk was growing from that pelvic organ cluster up into the pod's ceiling. And there were about 3 inches of the stalk buried underground when you first found it, right?"

"Mm-hm…" I hum, desperately trying not to puke again.

"Okay, and the stalk was, what, 4 inches from the mound to the flower? And from the petals to the tip of the phallus, you said it was eight inches?"

"Yup, that's about right."

"Okay, so that would mean that man had a 17-inch cock…"

"Or…" I mutter. "Or maybe the organism merged with the guy's penis after he tried to fuck the fleshy hole in the middle of the yoni flower, then it encased the rest of his body inside the pod before dissolving him for food until it had enough organic material to a grow a stock beneath the penis that it assimilated with, pushing it up through the soil into the open air for my dumbass to find…"

"What's crazy is how that makes perfect sense…" Priya says, shaking her head. "I guess the real question is, how did the body get here in the middle of this tree?" she says, looking around. "Did he, like, die here while taking shelter in the hollow?"

I shrug. "That, or someone buried him here…"

"Maybe they buried him after killing him when they saw what was happening to his body…" Julie mutters with a sour expression. "Like, maybe gross, slime mold skin that looked like this pod rind was spreading all over him, so they got scared and buried him where no one would ever come across the infected body."

"I could totally see that happening…" I say, my words trailing off. That's when it hits me…

This flower not only merged with my vagina and the surrounding skin, but it also turned my uterus into something that looks just like this pod… Does that mean it will eventually encase my entire body like it did to this corpse?

The thought petrifies me and makes my heart race harder than it ever has before.

"I wonder how long he's been here…" Priya says, snapping me out of my nightmare of a thought.

I gulp hard. "This poor guy could've been here for a few months, or he could have been here since the first Native Americas came to this rainforest…"

"You're not wrong…" Priya says. "It looked like the organs with the ejaculate stuff was nestled in the hip bones, like it needs it for structural support."

Just like how my corrupted uterus with that same pear-shaped, sap-containing organ is nestled in my pelvis…

I shiver. "I think the real question we should be asking is: where did he first encounter the yoni flower before he ended up in this hollow? Was the original yoni flower from this rainforest or from somewhere else?"

"You mean somewhere like a meteor from outer space, right?" Priya says with a nervous smile.

I snicker nervously. "At this point, anything is possible… Especially when this thing had matches with human, plant, and fungus genes with the majority of them not being similar to anything we as a species have sequenced yet…"

"So…" Julie says, turning back to the uncovered pod. "What do we do now?"

I huff. "I think we need to dissect the pod like a cadaver and take those bones as samples. Maybe we can use his DNA to find some living relatives and figure out where he came from."

"Um, what?" Priya says, gagging.

"No, Allie is right," Julie says, nodding. "If we can extract DNA directly from his marrow, we can use one of the genealogy sites to find familial matches and region-specific DNA."

Priya shakes her head. "Fine. Let me just brush my teeth and get this vomit taste out of my mouth, then we can dissect away…" She starts marching back to the tent with us at her heels.

CHAPTER 13
INSIDE THE YONI'S POD

Saturday

"Alright," Priya says, pulling her hoody down over her bikini top. "Let's get this over with…"

Julie, who's still wearing nothing but her army green, two-piece swimsuit, pulls the waistband of Priya's black bikini bottoms then releases it, letting it snap against her hip. "What, no pants, Pri?"

"It's too warm for pants *and* a hoody."

"It's too warm for just a hoody!" Julie fires back.

"True, but I'd rather get stains on my hoody than on my one good shirt. And I figured my arms were more likely to get yoni pod goo on them than my legs are, so this," Priya pauses to gesture to herself from top to bottom, "was the compromise."

Julie looks down at her bare arms then glances at me right as I'm buttoning up my brown long sleeve. "Yeah… smart… Since I don't feel like putting more clothes on or getting slime on my favorite hiking shirt, I'll just leave all the bone and root harvesting to you and Allie then." She says with a grin, tugging my sleeve.

"Fine," I say, "you're on film duty then."

With a fresh pair of gloves on, I kneel before the bottom side of the pod near where I cut the hole into the rind, then I draw my survival knife from the sheath. "Alrighty…" I take a deep breath then exhale slowly. "Here we go." Slowly, I drive the tip of the blade into the dense meat and it slides in like butter. It makes me cringe because it feels like I'm stabbing someone.

The oval flesh-sarcophagus is about six feet long and close to two feet across, so I start cutting a rectangular flap about a foot from the bottom and three inches from the side of the pod. With Julie guiding me using the endoscope, I carve all the way up to where the rib cage was suspended from the top of the pod.

About a foot from the top, I set aside my slimy knife then grab the thick flap of rind with two hands while Priya does the same on the other side of the pit.

"On three?" I ask.

Priya nods.

"One…" I begin. "Two… Three!"

The large flap separates from the rest of the pod with a gross, sticky, *schlick* of a sound that reminds me of a spoon stirring creamy mac and cheese. About a quarter of the way into peeling back the surprisingly heavy flesh door, the *organs* and the pelvis bone surrounding the internal part of the stalk comes into view with wormlike veins dangling from them. I gag when I see the translucent, yellow tissue that's fastening the pelvis bones to the underside of the pod flap. Then I dry heave again when I see the suspended spine swaying beneath the flesh door. The spine goes from the hip bones through the rib cage, and then it bends under the part of the flap that I didn't cut away, leading into a…

"That's a fucking skull inside the pod!" I blurt out in shock, staring that the membrane-encased, rounded bone that's dripping with brown slime.

Julie, who's been recording the dissection with her fancy Nikon camera, zooms in on it. "Umm… I think you're right… and I'm pretty sure there's something like a brain inside of it…"

"No way…" I gasp.

Priya and I rest the pod flap against the soil pile at the top of the pit, placing two shovels on it to weigh it down.

Kneeling beside Julie, I stare in horror through the opening in the base of the skull at this wrinkled, brain-like mass encased by a translucent, yellow membrane that's connecting it to the dangling tip of the spinal cord. "Holy fuck…" I say in awe.

Priya then squats across the pod from us and looks underneath the skull. "It looks like a giant Gyromitra esculenta—the brain mushroom. But this is *way* bigger than that species—bigger than a human brain."

"Oh God…" Julie whimpers. "Do you think it can feel pain?"

Guilt pangs in my gut. "It's possible… I mean, my petals were able to feel pain as soon as the flower merged with me, so…"

"The question we should ask is: is it conscious?" Priya asks.

"No clue," I say with a shrug. "But do you all see these thin, branched lines spreading outward from the pelvis bones and the spine?" I point to the symmetrical, organized web of thin roots that are covering the underside of the flap and weave overtop the veins and such. "What does that look like to you?"

"Neurons…" Priya gasps.

"Yeah…" Julie whispers. "You ever see the display at the Museum of Osteopathic Medicine A.T. Still University? These two students spent something like 1500 hours dissecting a cadaver and cut out an in-tact nervous system in 1925, then they preserved it and had it put on display in the museum."

"Sounds familiar," I say, thinking back to the one bio class where the professor showed us a complete map of a human's neurons spread across a brown background in a picture frame.

"Well, it looks exactly like that," Julie says, gagging again.

"This thing is unreal…" I say, shaking my head as I think about how this organism used some dead guy's hijacked organs and nervous system to ejaculate inside who knows what inside of me…

And then I remember the oval, lychee-like objects in the sac I found buried towards the base of the stalk. *They didn't taste like fruit because they weren't fruit or seeds… they were… actual testicles… Mutated ones…* I think about how the flower's jizz corrupted my eggs, turning them into those grape-sized things that I birthed last night. It makes me wonder if the plant's testicles pumped out some kind of mutated sperm that it used to *fertilize* my eggs…

"Unreal and *really* fucking disturbing…" Priya mutters. "Let's hurry up and get our samples, close this pod back up, and bury it forever so we can get to work suppressing this memory for the rest of our lives."

"Agreed," I say with a nod. "I'll collect some bones and organ samples."

"And I'll harvest some roots and veins…" Priya groans, gagging after.

Doing my best not to puke, I kneel before the pod flap and grab hold of a rib. Whatever the gelatinous tissue is that's holding the bones to this pod, it is incredibly strong. I have to slice it a few times just to get it to tear away. Even then, it takes everything that I have to rip it away from the pod's fleshy flap. And when the bone breaks away from the rest of the ribcage with a loud snap, I throw up a little.

"Oh god…" Julie groans, covering her mouth with her hand.

"Things aren't that pretty over here either," Priya says, wincing and groaning as she uses the thick branch that she found near the edge of the clearing to lift a tangled mass of slime-dripping roots and fleshy cords out of the pod.

As I'm bagging the second rib that I just broke off, I watch Priya struggle to pry the roots and veins up out of the goo. After shifting her feet to get a better stance, she lifts and pulls the branch towards her with one hard, fluid motion. And that's when I see the soil beneath her feet shift and avalanche into the pod.

"Priya! Get back!" I shout.

But it's too late, the soft dirt crumbles away in a massive chunk, sending Priya toppling into the pod, landing face-first into the slime with a thick, bloop of a splash.

"Priya!" Julie and I shout, running over to her side of the pit as she flails in a panic while quickly sinking into the amber syrup.

By the time we reach out to grab her, Priya's completely submerged. I can just barely see her thrashing around in the roots and veins that she's tangled up in. Without missing a beat, Julie drops to her knees right beside where the soil caved in then plunges her bare arm into the pool of goo before I can get my fear-paralyzed body to move.

"Grab hold of me, Allie!" Julie screams.

I wrap my arms around her skinny waist and lean back.

Unfortunately, Julie just misses Priya's hand, then we wind up watching our friend as she sinks further into the viscous liquid, disappearing into the darkness. Julie looks at me in horror and, right as she's about to dive in after her, Priya suddenly reappears from the dark mid-layer, her hand breaking the slime's surface before her head does in the next second. Even though Priya looks like she's standing now, she's still shoulder-deep in the muck, which makes sense considering she's only five feet tall and this pod is about four feet deep.

Priya coughs up a mouth full of dark amber gunk then gasps for air with a "GWAAUUH!" sound, one hand blindly reaching around for us while the other frantically wipes away slime from her eyes. "Help!" she mewls, spewing more goo afterward.

The second Julie grabs her hand, I pull her with everything I've got only for Priya's extremely slick hand to slip through her grip, resulting in both of us falling backward onto the soil.

"I'm stuck on something!" Priya coughs violently, thick strings of what looks like maple syrup swaying from her mouth and chin.

She reaches down and pulls at the dark woody cords wrapped around her torso. "These roots are tangled in my fucking bikini bottoms. Ow! There are hooks on them, and they're caught in my hoody too!"

"Shit…" I mutter. "You might have to strip so we can pull you out!"

"Okay, yeah. Good thinking," she says, wiping her eyes again. "Can someone grab me a towel?"

"I'm on it!" I run around the pit to the tent.

"What's it feel like in there?" I hear Julie ask her.

"Uh, well… it's like swimming in warm syrup—syrup that's sweet, super salty, and a bit funky tasting. Uh, the floor is squishy like the top layer of the pod. Super slippery too. And the gunk layered on the floor is chunky like mashed potatoes… Also, this sharp web of roots I'm tangled up in keeps scratching me. Oh, and not only do I have veins that feel like giant worms rubbing against my limbs, but I've got the pinecone bulb of one of those hairy, giant asparagus-things pressing right up against my fucking crotch…"

"Does it feel good?" Julie asks.

"Fuck you, Julie!" Priya shouts. "Why don't you come in here and find out?"

"Here's your towel, Priya," I say, shaking my head at Julie as I extend the towel to our friend.

"What? I was trying to make her laugh…" Julie says quietly.

"Thanks, Allie," Priya says after blindly grabbing the towel from me following three failed attempts. After vigorously wiping her face, Priya peeks at me through squinted eyes. "Much better."

"Does it burn your eyes?" I ask.

"A little… No worse than pool water, I guess…" Priya hands the sticky towel back to me then reaches down into the slime with both hands. "Crap… These roots are legit woven through my bikini bottoms like barbed wire… And I swear it feels like they are snaking across me and wrapping tighter."

"It's all in your head," I tell her, even though I know all too well that this thing is probably capable of moving its internal organs since its phallus throbbed as soon as sensed my touch.

And it did ejaculate in me after excessive stimulation, so…

"No, it's not in my head. I'm standing still and I feel them moving." Priya jumps. "Geez! It's not just the roots, it feels like that stalk between my legs is brushing its pinecone bulb back and forth against my you know what! And the one by my leg feels like it's slithering around my knee like a snake!"

I watch through the murky slime as Priya frantically wriggles her bottoms down as far as the tangled mess of woody roots will let her. *It makes sense that the internal appendages can move if the linga phallus responded to touch, especially if they have sticky hairs like the sundew because those plants move to trap prey…*

Is this thing trying to wrap her up and digest her? Is this some sort of defensive mechanism for anything that enters the pod?

Out of nowhere, she jerks and flinches. "Ow!"

"What?" I scream.

"When I tried removing the thing curling around my left leg, it pulled my skin or something! I need to get the fuck out of here!" Her bottoms are stuck just above her knees now, so she gives up on trying to pull them down any further and just tries lifting a leg up through the hole. She manages to pull her left foot through but, right as she's bringing her foot back down, she loses her balance and catches herself in a sort of split with her head back and her face barely above the surface of the slime. "AHHH!" she shrieks louder than I've heard anyone scream before.

"What happened?!" I shout.

Priya slips again then starts thrashing around and screaming bloody murder as she struggles to regain her footing—struggling like someone trying to stand on a hill covered in black ice. "Oh god! AHHH!" she screeches. "Oh god no!"

"Priya, talk to us!" I shout. "What's happening?!"

"AH…." She winces and, after a bit more thrashing, she manages to stand upright, one hand still reaching down in between her legs, her eyes widening with terror. "Fuck…"

"What?" Julie and I shout.

"That the fist-sized pinecone bulb of the stalk—ah…" She flinches again, fidgeting with the thing between her legs. "It's inside of me!"

"Um, what do you mean *inside* of you?" Julie asks.

"What do you *think* I mean, Julie?" Priya screams. "I *literally* just told you that the bulb was brushing against my coochie, so what do you *think* happens when someone in a pit of forbidden lube accidentally falls into a split *right on top of* a smooth, rounded spear tip?! That's right, it glides right into your birth canal!"

"Oh shit…" Julie mutters, covering her mouth.

"Oh shit," I echo. "How far in is it?"

She groans. "Oh, it's *in* there. Like, *all the way* up against my cervix in there!" Through the sludge, I can barely see her grabbing the stalk and giving it a little tug. "Fuck! I can't get it out!" She tries again then flinches so hard that her body spasms. "OW! Fuck!"

"What?" I cry out. "Is it swelling inside of you?"

"Oh god!" she whimpers. "No! Whenever I try tugging it out, the spines under the bulb pull my labia!" She fidgets a bit. "Ah-AH! Shit! My hand!" She winces then lifts her arm out of the slime, staring at her palm. Even through the glaze coating her hand, I can see that she's missing patches of skin.

"What's happening to your hand now?" Julie asks as Priya.

"I think it's the quills sticking out of the stalk…" Priya says. "They don't hurt to touch because they're rubbery with blunt ends, but it hurt like hell when I tore my hand away just now! It hurt the same way it hurt when I tried getting the one off my leg!"

"Priya," I say as calmly as possible, "Those little orange balls at the ends of the *quills*? I think they're just like the sticky ends of the sundew plant's tentacles—the gluey globs they catch prey with…"

Priya's eyes go wide. "Oh god… so those quills underneath the base of the bulb are glued to my labia too?! Fuck! Fuck me!" Priya starts sobbing, trembling as she does.

My eyes widen as I slip into shock. My body goes rigid.

"What're we gonna do?" Julie whispers to me.

"Something's wrong," Priya whimpers, sniffling after. "I'm starting to feel really drowsy all of the sudden. I need to get out! Now!"

"Fuck it, I'm going in," Julie says, undoing her bikini top.

"What?" I blurt out, my body still frozen.

"No!" Priya cries. "You're just going to get stuck too, then that'll be two of us trapped in here for this thing to sedate and liquify!" Her sobbing resumes.

Julie tosses her top. "The roots can't get stuck on my clothes if there's nothing to get snagged onto!" she says, yanking down her bikini bottoms and stepping out of them. She sits her bare ass on the edge of the pit then dips her feet into the slime before easing herself in slowly. "Oof! That's warm… and *thick*… This is what I imagine soaking in a hot tub full of cum is like."

"Gross…" I mutter. "Julie, *please* be careful!"

"I'll be fine, Allie," she says, looking up at me as she high-steps her way through the sludge pool and the web of cords towards Priya. "Just get ready to pull Priya out as soon as we get this hoody off of her, okay?"

I nod.

"Raise your arms for me, Pri," Julie says to her.

One by one, Julie begins removing the root's barbed ends from the front and sides of Priya's hoody. "Okay, that should be good." She grabs the hoody by the sleeves then pulls it up over Priya's head only for it to stop halfway.

"There's still a few barbs snagged the back of the hoody!" I announce.

"Damn it," Julie says inspecting her back. "Priya, lean forward. I'm just going to rip it free with one hard yank, okay?"

"Okay," Priya responds.

When she leans forward, Julie takes a step back and tugs it with everything she's got. As hoody finally tears away from the roots, Julie falls backward into the slime with a loud bloop, sinking near the bottom end of the pod a foot from where the stalk was.

"Julie!" I shout, plunging my arm into the warm sludge.

In the midst of her thrashing, Julie's fingers brush against mine briefly before she sinks further into the depths of the pod in slow motion. In a matter of seconds, she disappears into the darkness at the bottom. Unlike Priya, she doesn't rise back to the surface. The only things that come up to the surface are a few big, slowly moving air bubbles.

"Priya, I don't see her!" I panic. "She should be back up by now! I'm going in after her!"

"No! Don't! All three of us don't need to get stuck in here, okay? Just hand me your knife. Since I can't pull this asparagus's pinecone out of me, I'll cut it at the stalk then I'll go down after her."

Nodding, I hand it to her, handle-side first.

Priya hunches forward, feverishly cutting away her bikini bottoms in a single slice before sawing at the pale stalk between her legs. "Finally!" she says after slicing through it. Right as she takes a cautious step forward, she stops abruptly. "What the—"

"What is it?"

"I didn't even realize that there's a stalk around my leg!" It's only when she lifts her right knee to her belly that I see another *tentacle* wrapped tightly around her calf and shin. She reaches back into the slime and starts sawing away at it.

"Priya, hurry! She's been down there a while!"

"For fucks' sake, I'm trying, Allie!" A few moments later, she slices through it. "Fucking finally." She says, tossing the slime-covered knife up to the ground beside me as she sloshes forward through the thickness, taking high and long steps to get over the roots. "I'm going under!" She takes a deep breath then submerges into the amber goo.

Time slows to a crawl. It feels like she's been down there for minutes before her silhouette finally rises from the darkness—her silhouette, and hers alone…

She bobs up through the surface with a gasp. "There's a hole!" she screams, panting as she blindly walks in my direction while reaching out for me. "Pull me out! There are more asparagus tentacles over here sticking to me!"

"Did you say *a hole*?" Using the towel, I wrap it around her slime-coated arm before grabbing her by the elbow and wrist, then I hoist her up out of the pod with everything I have.

When her legs leave the goo pool, her bare breasts mash into my chest as she collapses right into me. Her weight topples me over then I hit the ground back-first with her slimy body on top of me. "Near the end of the pod—" she says, panting hard as she rolls off of me. "There's a hole!"

"What do you mean there's a hole? In the floor of the pod?"

Priya nods while wiping her face with the towel. "I was on my hands and knees feeling around in the roots for Julie, and the floor on that side was just fucking not there! I reached in past my elbow and nothing, Allie! I didn't feel her anywhere down there!"

My eyes widen as I spring up. "Holy shit! Holy shit! Holy fucking shit!" I climb to my feet and start pacing. "We have to get her!"

"How?" Priya shouts, crying. "If I stuck half my arm in and couldn't even reach the top of her head, that means the hole's depth is over the length of her body! That's over 5 feet! And it's not like you can swim in that stuff! We go down there; we're not coming back up! Not with those roots and adhesive stalks down there!"

"So, what?" I shout, pacing back and forth. "We leave Julie down there to drown in the fucking yoni pod slime, Priya?"

"You think I don't want to try to save her? I'm *telling you* that there's no way for us to safely get her *and* return to the surface if there's no floor to push off of!"

I snap my fingers. "What about a rope?! There's 100-feet of rope in my pack!" I race around the pit toward the tent.

"Allie—"

"You can tie a rope around me, I can dive down, then you can pull us up when you feel me tug it!" I interrupt.

"Allie, look at my fucking leg!"

A few feet from the tent, I spin around, staring in horror at what she's pointing at. I was so busy freaking out over Julie disappearing into a tunnel or whatever that I didn't even notice the off-white stalk covered with thick, black quills that's coiled tightly around her right leg like a boa constrictor.

The once straight vine is now wrapped around her limb just like how sundew plants roll up around insect prey...

And then my gaze falls between her spread legs—the reason she can't stand normally with her legs together. Not only is her vagina stretched open by the pinecone-shaped bulb stuffed inside of her, but the severed stalk still attached to the bulb's base is clung to the inside of her left thigh like a sea urchin.

I didn't realize how thick those freaky tentacle stalks were… The one around her leg is maybe 1.5-inches in diameter, which means the more bulb in her vagina is probably closer to 2 inches wide… And those black spines on the stalk… they're as thick as hedgehog quills!

She sniffles. "Look!" Using the towel, she grabs the hairy vine coiled around her leg. When she tries pulling it away, her skin stretches with it. "These orange balls at the end of the hairs are fucking glued to me! If you go into the tunnel and these asparagus vines are down there too, they're going to wrap around you and there's no pulling them off, Allie! And you can't see down there, so it's not like you can cut yourself free the way I did."

I blink rapidly. "We have to try something, Priya! We have to!"

Priya sobs. "Allie… I want to save her as badly as you do, you know I do! But it's already been nearly two minutes… If she hasn't drowned already, she'll be out of air before we could safely find her and get her out…"

With wide, unblinking eyes, I collapse onto my knees beside the base of the pod. "I don't believe this…"

"I don't believe it either…" Her crying intensifies. "It feels like a fucking nightmare…"

"It's all my fault," I say, staring at the pod shaking my head as my vision blurs with a wall of tears. "I should've never brought you two here!"

"Your fault?!" Priya screams. "She jumped in there to save *me!* Because I fell in! I felt the ground shift under my feet, Allie! I felt it and I ignored it because I thought I was close to ripping the roots out!" She buries her face in her palms then sobs. 'She's dead because of me!"

Unsure of what to say, I just crawl over to Priya then I wrap my arms around her slick body. Eventually, she leans her naked form against me, then we both just break down, weeping and sniveling uncontrollably. The entire time, I stare over her head at the pool of slime, hoping that Julie will break through the surface.

She and I stay there crying like that for a long while until she suddenly begins trembling against me.

"Priya, you're shivering…" I whisper.

"I just got so cold all of the sudden…"

Hearing that makes me think back to the fever I had after the yoni flower got stuck in me. "Come on, let's take care of these vine-things, get that bulb out of you, and get you cleaned up so we can get some clothes on you, okay?"

She nods against my bosom. When we part, chunky ropes of thickened mucus stretch between her face and my shirt. "Yeah… I was about to say… I *really* need to get these vines off… It's starting to burn… where the stalks are touching… my skin," she speaks with frequent pauses like her breath is labored. Her eyelids are at half-mast like she's seconds from passing out.

Now panic really sets in, because all I can think about is the burning that I felt when the spadix heated up inside my vagina before it fused to me. "Don't worry," I say calmly as I rise to my feet, "I'll get them off of you and you'll feel better in no time, okay?"

She nods weakly, wincing.

The moment I take her hand to help her up, my gaze falls onto her right leg and my jaw drops. It takes everything not to gasp.

What? No… Please tell me I'm seeing things…

From where I'm standing, it looks like the stalk's thick quills aren't just pressed *against* her flesh like they were a bit ago, they look like they've grown *into* her. Like, a black thread has sprouted from the tip and has grown under her mocha skin now, spidering a few centimeters up and down from the points of contact like skinny, black, varicose veins…

No… Don't tell me they're rooting into her…

CHAPTER 14
YONI POD EXPOSURE

Saturday

To keep the four inches of the stalk that's still sticking out of her vagina from adhering to the other thigh, Priya has to shuffle-waddle to the tent in a partial squat.

The second I help her ease down onto Julie's sleeping bag, she waves me off. "It's okay, she groans, "I can lay down on my own."

Nodding, I quickly kneel before her, reach over to grab my pack, and then I rummage through it until I find my first aid pouch. Like Priya's body, my trembling hands are sticky with the thickening pod slime, so it's a struggle to get these latex gloves on. After failing to pull the first glove on, I use some soap, a cloth, and water from my bottle to scrub my hands. Now the first glove goes on with ease. While pulling on the second glove, I look over at Priya. She's laying on her back in the hook lying position—feet flat on the floor with her bent knees pointing to the tent's ceiling—and her legs spread wide open like she's ready to give birth.

I can't look away, I think, staring at how freaky her hairless vagina looks with that tentacle stuffed in her. The way that white stalk looks coming out of her splayed open labia, the way the bulb is bugling behind her pussy lips like a giant, white onion is stuffed in her... *It looks like she's birthing some horrible, albino snake, tail-first...*

It's only when I position myself right between her knees and lean in that I realize her labia are extremely swollen. Not only are they swollen, but black threads are growing outward under her skin from where the orange balls at the ends of the quills are stuck to her flesh. There's also some kind of pink goo dripping out of the severed end of the stalk…

Whatever is dripping out of the stalk reminds me of the gunk that my yoni flower excreted that first night. Dissolved vaginal and uterine flesh… I hope it's not that, I think, wrapping my hand around the four inches of stalk sticking out of her vagina.

To my surprise, the quills are soft and bendable, like silicone spikes. And the tentacle I'm now squeezing feels like a spongey, flexed muscle. When I try taking my hand off of it, the clear, orange balls on the tips of the quills stretch my glove away from my hand.

Then, when I try lifting the stalk a bit to see how stuck it is, Priya jumps. "Ah! HRRNNG…" she groans.

"Sorry!" I squeal, grabbing my medical scissors with my free hand. "Alright, Priya… I think the only way to get this off is to cut the quills away from the stalk. After that, I'll try pulling the hairs out one by one, okay?"

"Just hurry, Allie…" she says sleepily. "It's itching and burning so bad… My whole body… it's itching too… I think I'm having an allergic reaction to the slime…"

I stare at the thickness coating my arms. *I'm not itching at all… Yet…*

Starting with the six rubbery quills rooted into her plumped labia, I snip them one by one. The first one that I cut leaks more of that pink goo that was coming out below. The second oozes something whitish-yellow, like pus the texture of mayo. Every other one I clip alternates between one of those two fluids.

"Alright," I say after snipping the last spine stuck to her vagina's opening, "I'm starting on the ones stuck to your thigh now then I'll move onto the big vine below your knee," I say as calmly as I can after seeing that the threadlike roots under her skin have grown another few centimeters since I started cutting.

Priya whimpers. "Can you pull the bulb out of me yet? It's so uncomfortable, and it feels like it's expanding."

Oh shit… I try slipping a finger into the slime oozing slit between the stalk and her swollen labia, but it's too tight of a fit. Also, because of the way this stalk is stuck to her inner thigh, there's no good angle to pull it out even if I could fit my fingers in. "Not yet. I have to get the rest of it off of your thigh first."

Just like with the ball-tipped *hairs* stuck to labia, each ruby spine stuck to her thigh that I cut drips something puslike or something pinkish-brown. There are over a dozen of them and, by the time I'm halfway through, I'm dripping sweat. If things weren't already bad enough, for some reason, each subsequent one I snip seems harder to cut than the last…

These are starting to feel more like wood than rubber, I think, straining to cut the third to last spine. The second to last one I cut snaps like a hard toenail.

"Ooooo-kay," I say, snipping the last one. Thick, snotty strings stretch between the stiffened stalk and her thigh as I pull it away. "Some of the hairs stuck to your labia are in the way, but I'm going to try and pull this thing out of you without hitting them, alright?"

"Yeah. Just get it out now, please! Something doesn't feel right!"

"Yeah! Okay! I'm going to slide two fingers into you so I can stretch you open a bit more, so this might feel a bit uncomfortable." Using the gloved hand stuck to the stalk, I pull the vine aside to the right then insert two fingers between the little gap between her extremely plump labia and the base of the bulb. My pointer and middle finger glide around the ribbed curve of the slimy bulb with the stickiest, creamiest of sounds.

"Ahhhh!" Priya moans as I shove my fingers into the second knuckle.

That's when I hit what feels like a thin, taut wire. *What the fuck was that?*

As slowly and gently as possible, I press the back of my fingers against her vaginal wall and stretch her open while pulling the hardening stalk with the other. With a bubbly spurt, the bulb begins sliding out, honey-colored sludge oozing out around it.

"GAHHH!" she cries, writhing as the girthy middle of the blub bulges through her opening.

"Almost there, Pri—" My words trail off when the beige, pinecone-like bulb the size of a small pear leaves her vagina with an unexpected sight as sludge gushes out of her gaped hole like snot.

Now that I'm seeing this rubbery-feeling bulb up close and personal, it totally reminds me of the Pinecone Ginger, or Zingiber zermumbet—a flower with a squishy, pinecone-like flowerhead composed of overlapping scale bracts that, when squeezed, produces an aromatic, slick liquid Hawaiians use as a shampoo.

The rubbery scales of this bulb aren't just unfurled like a fully opened pinecone now, there are also these thin black fibers stretched between the gapped bracts and the interior walls of her gaped vagina. And, from the center of the bulb's tip, there is a taut, black tendril that's anchored somewhere deep inside of her. It's only after bringing the lantern up to her vagina that I realize the tendril goes all the way into her inflamed cervix. Also, her cervix, her reddened vaginal walls—the stringy roots have rooted under her tender flesh just like the stalk's bendy quills have done to her labia and legs… Like, it's so bad that it looks as though someone tattooed the inside of her pussy with black veins…

Oh no… you've got to be shitting me, I think, peering inside her still gaped vagina that won't snap shut for some reason. *I've got to get these roots out of her vagina…* Holding the flashlight outside of her opening, I slowly pull on the stalk until the hairy roots begin snapping away from her vaginal walls while the black, spaghetti-thick cord drags out of the cervical hole like a shoelace from a puckered anus.

"AAAARGH!" Priya cries as the tendril in her cervix goes taut. "Fuck! Allie, why does it hurt? Oh God!"

"Priya… Part of it is stuck in your cervix. I need to pull it out, so ball up that shirt next to you and bite down on it, okay."

Nodding, she grabs the shirt and stuffs it into her mouth. When she's ready, she gives me a thumb's up.

With the flashlight in my mouth and the stalk still in my right hand, I pinch the tendril with my free fingers and pull the black noodle with more and more force until it starts sliding through the pinhole again. Eventually, her cervical os stretches open a bit as something inside starts bulging through.

"MMM-MMMMRGH!" she growls through the shirt gag. With one moderately hard tug, a tight cluster of slimy roots the size and shape of a black bean pops out, blood and something white like yogurt dripping out of her cervix. "AHHH!" Her core spasms when it leaves her, forcing out another big spurt of thickened pod slime from her gaped coochie.

"I got it out, Priya!" I shout, removing my right glove so I can drop what I just pulled out of her into the container beside me. "It's out!"

She sits up a bit, pulling the shirt out of her mouth. "What was that?" she asks weakly, panting for air.

"A root of some kind that sprouted out of it. Don't worry about it. Just lay back so I can pull these quill-things out of you."

After putting on a fresh pair of gloves, I pinch one of the black spines stuck in the opening of her vagina then give it a gentle tug. Her engorged vaginal fold stretches with the stalk's severed quill and, when her flesh can't stretch any further, the rubbery spine budges just a bit only for her to scream bloody murder.

"AAHH! Shit! Stop! Stop!" she cries, flailing her legs so wildly that she almost kicks me. "Just…" She pauses to pant. "Just fucking leave it, Allie! It feels like you're trying to rip my skin off!"

I release the hardened spine. "Okay! Okay! Sorry! I'll just work on getting the last vine off of your leg!"

"Wait, is there still something in there?" she asks, pointing at her vagina. "I feel… *stuffed* or something."

I slip a finger into her still gaped labia, pull her open a bit, then shine the flashlight inside, her reddened walls and the pool of slime inside of her canal glinting from the light. "There's still a lot of slime in there…"

"That's it? It feels like there's a whole mango in there or something… Is there a way to get the slime out?"

"I can try scooping it out with my fingers? Or maybe a travel spoon?"

"You know what? Forget it. This vine feels way worse. Just get that off of me please."

"Yeah, you got it!"

Holy shit, I think, looking at her leg. *The black roots under her skin have grown almost an inch across her leg since the last time I checked… This is not good…*

Unlike the pinecone bulb that I pulled out of her vagina, the one pressed against her leg isn't unfurled and there aren't roots growing out from between its bracts either…

Weird… Maybe it only sprouts roots when it's inside of its prey? Or maybe, like the linga phallus, it behaves differently when exposed to vaginal fluids…

The vine coiled below her knee isn't off-white anymore like it was when she first emerged from the pod, it's a light brown now. And when I curl my fingers around the stalk, it doesn't feel like a flexed muscle the way the one coming out of her vagina did. This one feels woody, like a branch. Also, not only are the spine's tips no longer sticky, but they also don't feel rubbery anymore. They're almost as hard stems now.

Holy shit, I wasn't wrong… these vines are turning woody like the rhizomorph roots inside the pod… Do these things curl around their prey, harden, and grow into new roots? Or are they turning woody because they're not attached to the pod and no longer inside the slime?

Snipping the hardened spines reminds me of pruning my rose bushes. Not only are there three times as many woody quills as there were on the last one but, because of the way this stalk is coiled around her calf and shin, the weird angles make it hard to reach certain spines. Some of them are so hard that it takes a few tries to cut through.

About a quarter of the way through snipping woody quills, rain begins beating against the part of the tent's roof that's not under the tree hollow. By the time I prune the final black quill, it sounds like there's a monsoon out there.

Since the stalk has basically petrified into a woody snake, I can't just unwrap it from around her leg. With trembling arms, I pry the coiled stalk apart until it snaps like a branch, leaking a syrupy, pinkish-brown liquid from one internal tube while the other *vein* drips something the texture and color of vanilla pudding.

I can't tell which of these fluids are coming out of her or which are being pumped into her by the stalk, I think, taking a closer look at the fleshy, muscle-like interior that reminds me of the inside of a fig, but tan in color.

"Alright," I say, tossing the woody vine into the bag with the other one, "the last stalk is off."

"Thank you so much," she says weakly, her voice wavering as her jaw trembles.

When she starts struggling to sit up, I take her hand and wrap an arm around her to help her up. "You're welcome…" I whisper. "But, before you look down, you should know that I couldn't get the quills out of your skin…"

"Out of my skin or off of my—" she stops abruptly and her sleepy eyes widen when she sees the nubs of the woody protrusions sticking out of her inner left thigh and below her right knee—when she sees the zigzagging, black threads branching out and spreading under her brown flesh. "Allie… Are—are these rhizomorphs growing under my skin?!" she shrieks, poking her thigh afterward. "Oh god! They are… Allie! Allie, what's happening?"

"I don't know, Priya…"

"Why didn't you tell me the hairs were growing under my fucking skin?"

"I didn't want you to panic while I was getting the vines off… And I tried to pull them out but you told me to stop… I'm sorry, Pri! I should've warned you!"

"Oh fuck, does that mean—" she touches her hand to her sticky vagina and jumps when she bumps the nubs protruding from her labia. "No…" She pulls one then jumps immediately after. "AH—HA-OW! What the fuck… Why does my vadge feel so full… and why is it all open and loose like this?" she asks, lightly tracing her gaped opening that looks like it's being held open by an invisible speculum. "Is there still something in there?"

I shake my head. "No… I pulled the bulb out. I think there's some kind of compound that's nullifying the elasticity of your vaginal walls… The phallus once made my vagina cramp around it, so I suppose these stalks could have a compound that can do the opposite."

Trembling, she plunges two fingers into her pussy and it makes the gushiest, stickiest, spurting sound. All sorts of squishy, squelching noises come out of her hole as she feels around. When she finally pulls her fingers out, there's a clump of something gelatinous that looks like white grape jelly jiggling in her trembling hand.

"What… is this…?" she asks, rubbing the gunk between her thumb and middle finger.

"I think the slime that the bulb pushed into you is coagulating, like the stuff glazed all over your body… Maybe that's why your vagina feels full and why it's not closing?"

"Oh gawd…" she wipes the gelatinous goo off onto the towel then fingers herself again, noisily scooping out a larger glob of yellowish jelly. "There's so much of it in there… There's no way *that* much slime got pushed into me." While she scratches her belly with her free hand, she continues scooping more goop out of her vagina, wiping it off on the towel after. Now she starts scratching her left tit. "Does that slime have you itchy too? It feels like bugs are crawling all over me!"

"I'm not itchy at all," I say, leaning closer when I see what looks like tiny bumps all over her belly. "Pri, I think you're breaking out in a rash…"

"Oh gawd… Allie… What's happening to me?"

Shaking my head, I rise to my feet. "I don't know… Could be an allergic reaction. Come on, let's go stand in the rain and wash this slime off before it hardens."

With a bottle of soap in one hand and a towel in the other, Priya prances around the pod on her toes then hurries out of the tree hollow into the torrential downpour. Once I'm done stripping, I stand there staring into the pod for a few moments, looking for signs of Julie before joining Priya in the rain.

Before tending to myself, I help wash her hair and scrub her back while she scrubs the rest of her body. It's only now that I'm helping her wash up that I notice her entire body is covered in a rash of some kind. A few bumps are bigger than the rest and filled with fluid like a blister. When I look down at the arm I dunked into the pod, I don't even find one bump.

Is my yoni flower keeping me from reacting adversely to the slime?

While Priya rinses off, she stands there in a partial squat, looking down between her legs as she fingers jiggling clump after jiggling clump of yellow-brown jelly out of her still swollen and gaped vagina.

That's a lot of muck she's scooping out… There shouldn't still be that much coming out of her, I think, scrubbing my arms.

After we're both done showering, we retreat into the tree hollow, Priya scratching herself along the way. Her body trembles violently as I towel her off outside the tent. As soon as I'm done, I touch the back of my hand to her neck and then her forehead. She should be cool after standing in the cold rain for almost twenty minutes, but…

"Priya, you're burning up!" I shout.

"Really? Because I'm freezing… I'm freezing and I feel like shit…" she says weakly, wrapping her arms around her body.

"Aside from being cold and itchy everywhere, do you have any other symptoms?" I ask, looking between her legs right as a glob of thickened slime starts stretching down from her gaped coochie like a snot tentacle. The sight makes me gag.

She blinks slowly and her body is swaying a bit. "Uh… I just feel super out of it…"

"Alright, this rain probably isn't going to let up for a while, so just bundle up, get into the sleeping bag, and rest until you have the strength to hike out of here, okay?"

With a sleepy nod, she turns and crawls into the tent.

Once I'm dried off, I put on my skirt, some long socks, a top, and a clean hoody, then I head into the tent to check on Priya. Not only is she burning up even worse than before, but her body is trembling so bad that she's almost convulsing. Also, the rash has spread to her face, and those bumps are starting to blister.

God, she looks like she has measles or something, I think, placing a damp rag on her forehead.

As worried as I am about her, I can't stop thinking about Julie—I can't stop the guilt from consuming me now that I'm not busy taking care of Priya.

Almost in a trance, I wander out of the tent then kneel before the bottom end of the pod, staring into the slime pit, watching as two little streams of rainwater drip into it. That's when I see the endoscope in the corner of my eye.

The cable is 16.4 feet long… Maybe I can feed it into the tunnel Julie fell into and find out how deep it really is.

The handheld is powered on before I feed the cable into the slime. Like last time, things get too murky to see, so I have to poke at the floor until I eventually find a spot where I can feed more of the fiberscope into the slime pool. It doesn't go straight down either. I can just barely see the fleshy, veiny tunnel curving under the ground where I'm standing. Somewhere around 8 feet deep, things get slightly less murky. This far into the tunnel, it's as clear as it is toward the top of the pod, maybe clearer. Fleshy veins and woody roots line the base of the tube with dozens of pinecone stalks fluttering up from the rind beneath them.

How did this thing grow a whole 'nother extension down here?

My guess? A root expanded over time and the fleshy encasing grew into it. Or maybe there's a small cave down there and the pod just expanded into it.

"Wait…" I whisper when I see what looks like a curtain of red fibers fluttering below. "What's that?" My eyes widen and my jaw hangs when I feed the camera another foot into the tunnel. "Oh God no… Those red fibers are… hairs…"

There, suspended in the middle of the tunnel in a tangled mess of roots, veins, and quill-covered stalks is Julie. Her eyes are bulging and her mouth is frozen open like she lost consciousness mid-scream. But I can't see into her mouth, because the pinecone bulb from the stalk above is stuffed behind her teeth. Not only is there one in her mouth, but there's also a bulb in her vagina, a stalk wrapped around her torso, and several *tentacles* coiled around her arms and legs…

"AHHHH!" I shriek, dropping the handheld display and scrambling back away from the pod in a crabwalk. My back hits the wall of the hollow and I clutch my knees to my chest, rocking back and forth, muttering, "Julie… no… no…"

I'm not sure how long I've been crying and rocking in the fetal position, but my joints are stiff and my ass is hurting from sitting on this lumpy soil for what feels like hours. The rain has also stopped at some point too.

Priya… I have to check on Priya… My knees still feel weak, so I basically crawl my way back to the tent. *She's still breathing,* I think, watching her chest rapidly rise and fall on my way to her.

She's drenched in sweat and she's still very warm to the touch, but it doesn't feel like her fever has gotten any worse. While the bumps on her hands are mostly fluid-filled, the ones on her face just look more like contact dermatitis now.

Doing my best not to wake her, I unzip her sleeping bag so I can take a look at her subdermal mycelium situation. *At least I think they're mycelium… they have to be if they grew that fast after initial contact…*

"Oh shit…" I whisper when I see that the black threads under her flesh have branched out more and spread another few inches.

How are they still growing even though they've been cut from the vine? My eyes wander to the quill nubs protruding out of her flesh that are oozing gooey, tapioca pudding stuff. *And what the fuck is that?* Every single spine I snip is oozing the same goop now. *It almost looks like liquid versions of pod rind … Don't tell me…*

"Oh god… is she being encased by the pod?"

Are these roots inside of her liquifying her?

I urgently peel away the sleeping bag and lift the skirt I gave her to wear. The blistering rash is all over her crotch too. Also, her vagina is still somehow gaped about two fingers wide, and there's a gross clump of yellow-brown jelly pooled between her legs with more of the liquid stuff running out of her like thin honey.

Geez, Priya… why are you still having jelly discharge? There shouldn't be any slime left…

Just like with the quill nubs on her legs, the ones around the inside of her labia are oozing some kind of pudding-like excretion. After putting on a glove, I click on my flashlight and shine it into her cavity as I'm pulling her open.

"Oh fuck!" I shout when the light illuminates a tangled mess of short, black strings growing out of her cervix.

Wait, it's not just growing out of her cervix, I think, shining the light onto her vaginal walls. There are thin, fur-like fibers growing out from the subdermal roots under her pink flesh.

"Pri!" I say, shaking her. "Priya, get up!"

"Hmm?" she moans without opening her eyes.

"Priya, it's done raining, you need to get up! We need to get you out of here and get you to a doctor ASAP!"

"I'm… too weak… right now… Let me just… rest a bit longer, Allie…" She's out cold before I can even respond.

Since it's not like I can carry her back to the trail, I guess I have no choice but to let her rest until she has the strength to walk… I turn to the pod. In the meantime, I need to seal that up…

Upon donning my fifth pair of gloves, I crawl out of the tent and pull all nine or ten feet of the endoscope out of the pod, trembling as the images of Julie flash in my mind. I don't even bother cleaning the cable, I just remove it from the handheld display and leave it on the ground. After that, I dunk the container with the bulb I pulled out of Priya into the slime to fill it up, then I snap the lid on and slip it into a sample bag. Once that's done, I lift the flap of the flesh sarcophagus back over the opening and release it, letting the heavy meat door slam shut with a disgusting splat.

It takes maybe an hour to bury the pod back up by myself. Once I'm finished, I gather up all of the gear and pack it away.

"Priya," I say, crawling back into the tent. I shake her by the shoulder hard, but she doesn't budge. "Priya, get up!" I scream.

At last, she jumps. "What?" she says groggily.

"We need to go! Now!' Up, up! Come on!"

"Allie, I'm still so tired and—"

"Priya, I know you're weak and out of it, but if we don't get you to a hospital before nightfall… it's not going to be good."

Her bloodshot eyes open halfway. "Is something wrong?"

"Yes. Your situation is getting worse, so you have to get up so we can get to a hospital!" I say, grabbing her hand and hoisting her up.

"Worse?" she whimpers. "Worse how?"

"I'll tell you on the way…"

It takes a bit but, eventually, Priya finds the strength to crawl out of our shelter and climb to her feet, with my help. We grab our packs and head out of the hollow, leaving the tent the way it is with Julie's gear still inside of it…

CHAPTER 15
13 MILES & A CAR RIDE

Saturday

The three-mile hike between the Hoh River trail and the Yoni Hollow clearing is what I'd describe as being moderate, and that's only because there are quite a few small obstacles, a lot of ducking under low hanging trees, a few steep declines on the way down, and there's not really a clear footpath to follow. For able-bodied individuals, it'd take an hour, tops. But when your travel companion is too shaky and weak to stand on her own, needs to take frequent stops, and is delirious with a fever, well, it takes a hell of a lot longer.

For the last 2.75 miles of our hike, Priya has had one limp arm draped over my shoulders and my arm has been wrapped tightly around her waist to keep her upright, so when her trembling body once again begins to collapse under her buckling knees, I stop abruptly and pull her against me. "Stay with me, Priya!" I shout, slapping her cheek when I see her drowsy eyes shutting slowly.

Priya shakes her head and blinks. "I just need another break…" she says weakly.

While I escort her over to a tree to rest against, I look up towards the sun peeking through the canopy ahead. "Okay, we can rest for a few minutes, but then we have to go, okay?"

She faces the moss-covered trunk then plants her arm against it and rests her forehead against her forearm. "I just wanna sleep…" she whines.

"I know, Pri, but we don't have time to sleep." I hand her my water bottle. "We've still got, like, a quarter-mile between us and the trail, then it's ten miles to the ranger station—that's another two-and-a-half-hours if we were walking at a moderate pace, which we are not doing, and we've barely got three hours of daylight left! If we don't hurry, we'll be caught in the dark. Then the temperature is going to drop, and you don't need to risk exposure to the cold and probably more rain on top of everything."

"I know… but…"

"No, *buts*, Priya! You're too sick. If you don't push through, you won't survive the night, you understand?"

She nods weakly against her arm.

"Okay, good," I say, rubbing her back. "Would you like me to help you sit down?"

"I don't know… if I can sit," she pants. "It feels like… something is hanging out of me *down there*…"

"Oh… I'm going to check under your skirt, alright?"

"Kay…"

The second I squat behind her—before I even lift her skirt, I see this viscous, glistening glob of amber slime swinging back and forth between her legs just past the hem. It's only after lifting her skirt that I notice the slime tentacle dangling out of her gaped vagina is clouded with milky white swirls. And that's not the only thing. Those fuzzy, black threads I saw inside of her cavity are now hanging out past her labia along with the pendulum of gunk.

This is not good… That's when I look down to her legs and find black fibers sticking out of the snipped stalk quills. *Ah shit… it's not just her vagina sprouting fibers…*

"Priya, can you hold your skirt up for me? There's more of that pod slime leaking out of you and I need to glove up and clean you up."

"Is it bad?" she asks, grabbing the hem of her skirt.

"There's just a lot of it…" I say, swinging off my pack and unzipping it.

It's only after riffling through my medical pouch that I realize I'm out of gloves. *Fuck it,* I think, grabbing a towel and slinging it over my shoulder.

With my hand cupped, I palm the tail end of the cold thickness and raise my hand towards her vagina to collect it all. And, when I reach her vulva, I use my fingers to scrape the stuff away from her clitoris towards her ass.

"Ah," she moans, quivering from my surprise touch of her intimate area.

This crap is so thick that, after I pinch it and yank it away from her cavity, it tears away like melted mozzarella cheese. It takes a few hard flicks of my wrist to get the slime to leave my hands.

"Bleh," I gag when it splats against the log beside us.

"Is it that bad?" she asks.

"It's just really thick now, that's… all…" My words trail off at the sight of this runnier, milkier goop that starts leaking out of her. "Priya, there's still more up there… I can—I can scoop it out if you want me to…"

"I can't ask that… of you… But it's probably a bad idea… to leave it inside of me… right?"

"Yeah… Alright…" As gently as possible, I spread her hot, swollen labia open with my left hand while bringing the pointer and middle finger of the other hand to her oozing entrance. "Here we go…" My digits plunge into her goo-filled hole with a loud squish.

Oh gawd… it's like fingering a pill bottle filled with clam chowder and Jell-O, I think, fighting the urge to gag as the musty gunk that I've just scooped out of her floods into my palm with a spurt.

"Mmm," Priya moans as I pump my fingers in and out of her again. I can't tell if she's uncomfortable or experiencing pleasure.

The longer I finger the filth out of her, the more the pool of thickness in my palm overflows. After a while, I start seeing bits of the black fibers floating in my hand. Before I know it, the hot sludge is running down my wrist and arm. *I hope I don't wind up with fibers growing out of my arm after this, I've already got enough wrong with me,* I think, involuntarily flexing the petals between my legs…

It takes nearly five minutes of scrapping her vaginal walls with curls of my fingers to empty the majority of the gunk out of her. When my sticky fingers leave her for the last time, only a few drops of cloudy goo drip down into my palm.

"I think that's as good as it's going to get, Pri," I say, watching the last drop fall from her dark brown pussy lip onto the cup's worth of thickness pooled in the soil below her.

"It feels a lot better now…" she pants. "Thanks… I know that was weird for you…"

"It wasn't *that* weird!" I say, pouring biodegradable soap onto my towel. "Besides, it's not like I didn't make you finger my yoni flower earlier this week."

She lets out a weak laugh as she sits down against the tree.

It takes even longer to scrub Priya's thick discharge off of me than it did to get the pod slime off, but at least there are no black mycelium fibers stuck to my skin when I'm done. *No fibers are growing out of my arm yet, at least,* I think, helping her up.

The dense brush we hike through after that isn't too difficult for Priya, but I know the muddy hill before us that leads down to the trail is going to be a bitch. We take it nice and slow, holding onto trees for support. Halfway down, I get one of those pleasant uterine spasms and I swear I feel another egg-thing working its way down into my yoni's canal. At that same moment, Priya slips, her wobbly legs give out, then she winds up dragging me down into the mud ass first.

As I sit up, I lift my skirt and flex my petals to check and see if something fell out of me during the fall. *If one of those eggs plopped out of me, I don't see anything in the mud below,* I think as I climb to my feet.

A few steps later, a yard from the base of the hill, she collapses again then we both fall onto a bed of ferns before tumbling through the rest of the brush, hitting the muddy trail with a thud.

I groan as I roll over in the muck. "You okay, Priya?"

"Yeah…" moans while trying to push herself up out of the puddle."

"You two alright?" a man's voice says from somewhere behind us right as I'm standing.

I twirl around and find two skinny thirty-somethings in raincoats hiking towards us. "My friend's sick!" I shout, helping Priya up. "Can you help me get her to the ranger station?"

The guys rush over to us.

"Yeah, of course!" one of them says.

"What's wrong with her?" the more muscular guy asks as he helps me get her onto her feet.

"Not sure," I mutter. "She's feverish and super out of it."

"Gotcha," he says. He then turns to his companion. "Topher, I'll stay with them. You run ahead and let the park rangers know we might need a medivac for this girl, okay?"

"Good call, Steve!" the skinnier guy says, racing off. "Hit me up on the walkie if anything changes!"

"No doubt!" Steve shouts back, turning to me. "If you don't mind carrying my pack, I can carry her on my back. It's not that heavy, we only packed for a day hike."

"Yeah, sure thing!"

Steve legit carries her almost the entire way back. Not long after we reached the end of the Hoh River trail, a medivac helicopter appears in the night sky and touches down in the clearing beside the ranger station. The medics check her vitals and hook her up to an IV while I explain to them and the park rangers how she fell into a puddle that had some sort of slime mold growing in it then had some sort of allergic reaction. That was the only thing I could come up with.

Then, while the medics are hauling her to the helicopter, I decide to inform the rangers that my friend Julie is still back at camp waiting for us because she wasn't with us while we were out exploring and has no idea that we had to get help. I figured it was better to tell them that now so they at least think she disappeared after we left rather than during. That's the only way I could think to keep the yoni-linga pod a secret without people thinking we murdered Julie. And I'd figure it'd buy us a day or two before I had to call in a search party.

The next thing I know, Priya was airlifted off to Tacoma General Hospital, leaving me to drive the three-hours-and-forty minutes there all alone, with no one or nothing to distract me from what happened to Julie and from what's happening to Priya.

As soon as I get in my car, I cross my arms against my steering wheel, rest my head against them, then I just break down, crying harder than I ever have in my entire life. *If I lose Priya too… I don't think I can live with myself…*

Three hours later, I see the signs for Olympia, Washington and, suddenly, I remember that me and Priya's backpacks have our yoni pod samples in them.

Shit… I should probably stop at home and get the samples in the freezer so they don't degrade any further. The last thing I want is for Priya's current predicament and Julie's sacrifice all to be in vain…

Wait, now that Julie's dead, who the hell's gonna take over her research into the Yoni pod samples? I supposed I can ask Catie Holden to take over…

Twenty-seven minutes later, I pull up to my house. With one pack slung over my shoulder and the other in my hand, I unlock the door then run down to the basement. Just as I'm putting the last of the slime-filled containers with the pod rind sample and the asparagus stalk in the deep freezer beside the bag of human ribs, my phone rings with a call from a number with a **(253)** area code.

That's a Tacoma area code… Maybe it's the hospital…

"Hello?" I answer.

"Good evening, this is nurse Stacia Burke from Tacoma General. Is this Priya Singh's friend, Allie Hannigan?"

"Yes, it is. Is Priya okay?" I almost yelp.

"She's stable now and her fever has come down some, but she did go tachycardic and lost consciousness following a seizure on the flight over."

"Oh, geez… A seizure?! Is she awake? May I speak to her?"

"I'm afraid not. She's still unconscious, but we'll let her know to call you as soon as she comes to."

"And what about those things growing in her leg and her privates?"

"From the preliminary lab results, the black fibers appear to be some type of mycelium, as you suspected, but it's unlike anything we've ever seen…"

"Are they still spreading?"

"Uh… I see here that the *roots* under her skin have grown approximately three inches since the EMTs last measured them on the helicopter… We're giving her antifungal medication to see if that helps. Then, once her temperature and blood pressure come down some, we're going to send her to the ER to see if we can excise them from her before they reach her organs."

My eyes go wide as I think about those black roots weaving around her major organs the way this one species of mold can do to immune-compromised individuals in rare cases of invasive aspergillosis. "Alright, is there anything else you can tell me, or is there anything else you need from me before I get to the hospital?"

"If you could tell me a little bit more about this fungus or slime mold, that might be helpful."

I spend another ten minutes on the phone with the nurse, giving her a vague description of the inside of the pod. Part of me feels like I should've just come clean about the pod and where it is or that I have samples for them to analyze, but something in my gut tells me that no one should have any contact with the yoni pod or its immortal phallus until I figure out what we're dealing with.

The last thing we need is an outbreak of those things…

Since Priya is stable, I hop in the shower instead of rushing right back out. I'm so burnt out by the time I finish drying off and getting dressed that I flop down on the bed to rest a bit while I catch up on all of my missed texts.

Of the twenty-five, unread texts, ten of them are from one contact: **Matty (One-Night-Stand guy)**. Three of his texts are from today.

Holy shit! I don't even remember exchanging numbers with him Thursday night… My heart starts racing before I even open his messages, because I know if he texted me this much in the last two days, that means the yoni egg that burst against his cock is still stuck to him. *Or it's spreading…*

Matty's 1st message Sent Friday at 1:30 a.m.: **Yo! WTF kind of STD did you have? This white shit is still plastered on my dick and I can't get it off!**

That message was sent two hours after I left his place Thursday night. And beneath that text, there's a picture of his flaccid dick, and it's covered in what looks like smeared buttercream icing from tip to about halfway down his shaft.

Oh fuck… I scrolly down.

Matty's 2nd message Sent Friday at 7:01 p.m.: **Yo! Seriously, I'm fucking scared now, Allison! Whatever this coating is on my dick, it's spreading! And not only has it spread, but I woke up with a boner this morning and it hasn't gone down since! Mind you, it's 7:00 p.m. now…**

Beneath that, there's a picture of his erection. Three-quarters of his member is coated in what looks like beige candle wax, and there are white, translucent, threadlike roots growing outwards from the edge of it toward the base of his penis and scrotum…

Matty's 3rd message Sent Saturday at 12:12 p.m.: **Um, so my doctor doesn't know what the fuck is wrong with my cock… He said he was going to have me tested for thrush? Did you give me a fungus? I can't find anything on the internet remotely resembling my situation… Care to shed some light on what's going on?**

Matty's 4th message Sent Saturday at 12:15 p.m.: **Oh, BTW, it's been over 24 hours and, not only has my boner still not gone down from the other day but there's this thick yellow stuff leaking out of the tip—because, for whatever reason, this shit is growing inside of my pee hole and my urethra is itching like a bitch!**

Matty's 5th message Sent Saturday 12:17 p.m.: **Did I mention I haven't peed since Friday night? Because I haven't. Also, this white fungus or whatever has spread from my dick to my balls! Fucking pick up your phone or text me back! Please! If we're both in danger, we need to figure this shit out! Please don't tell me you're not responding because you're dead…**

Another boner picture is below that. The beige, waxy flesh growing over his cock resembles the spadix phallus even more now, and the white, icing-looking skin has grown down to the underside of his testicles…

The rest of his texts are a lot of threats followed by apologies for coming off hostile. There's also an offer to meet and talk about what's happening to him.

All I can imagine is the white stuff spreading across his entire body, eventually turning him into another pod.

Oh god… I have to figure out what to do about Matty before he dies…

If he dies, they'll trace his condition back to me…

If they trace it back to me, I'll get taken into some laboratory black site and the government is going to study me and keep me quarantined for the rest of my life… Then the same thing will happen to Priya…

My chest heaves rapidly as I start hyperventilating. My body trembles violently.

Oh god… what have I done?

CHAPTER 16
THE LINGA STAGE

Sunday

Numb. I'm just so numb.

Shortly after reading all of Matty's texts last night, I laid there under the covers sobbing for hours before eventually crying myself to sleep. But I didn't stay asleep. If I wasn't woken up by the reoccurring nightmare of watching Julie sink into yoni pod only for me to find her dead body suspended in syrup with tentacle stalks stuffed in her orifices, it was the dream of Priya's body being rapidly taken over by the black rhizomorphs that had me spring up in a cold sweat. Now it's almost noon and I'm still curled up in fetal position under my blanket, my unblinking eyes staring into my dark closet. I'm too numb to cry anymore and too high-strung to sleep even though I desperately want to.

As I've done every few hours since last night, I pull down my blanket and look at my arms, checking them for a rash and for those black fibers that Priya had growing under her flesh. *Still clear,* I think, caressing my smooth, uncorrupted skin. *At least I don't have to worry about rhizomorphs growing in me on top of everything else,* I think as I pull the covers back up. *The question is, why? Did merging with the yoni flower provide me with immunity to the negative effects of the stuff inside the pod? Have I become more like a walking yoni flower and less of a woman?*

The buzzing of my phone on the nightstand snaps me out of the thought and I reach out to grab it without missing a beat, only because it might be Priya.

Oh, it's Catie, I think, unlocking my phone and opening the Facebook chat bubble.

Since I didn't have her number, I messaged Julie's grad school lab partner on here this morning with: **Hey, Catie! Julie told me you've been helping with the sequencing/IDing of the samples from that weird organism we found, so thanks for your help!**

She may or may not have told you, but we went hiking this weekend in Hoh Rainforest to obtain some more samples from the organism. Unfortunately, when Priya and I went exploring on our own yesterday, Pri had an accident and got really sick so I had to rush her to the ranger station, leaving Julie back at camp with no idea that we left. Now it's Sunday and Julie still hasn't contacted us yet, so I'm worried that she may have gotten lost out there (since we were off-trail miles from a designated campsite).

Since the organism we're studying is a part of the reason Priya is in the hospital, it is critical that we get the samples analyzed ASAP. So, can I drop them off with you to get started on while I head back to Olympic Nation Park to find Julie?

Catie responded to that with: **OMG! I'm so sorry to hear about Priya! Tell her she's in my thoughts! And I really hope Julie is okay! I'm sure you'll find her if she doesn't call you soon. You know our favorite ginger, she's more of the type to sit and wait for help than someone who'd roam the wilderness alone to find civilization haha.**

But yes, you can drop off the samples. I'll actually be at the lab today around 3:00 p.m. to redo a PCR test if you want to come by then.

Even though I'm too depressed about my dearly departed best friend and too worried about Priya to even want to get out of bed and eat today, that message convinces me to get up and drive my ass to Seattle. Because figuring out what this yoni flower and its pod innards are made of could be what leads to a way to save Priya.

All I can think about now that I'm back in Seattle is Matty and what he's going through because I couldn't keep my flower in my pants. The fact that he's gone from spamming me every few hours to zero calls and texts after last night, it makes me worry that something awful has happened to him. I can't help but picture someone walking into his apartment and finding a gross flesh sarcophagus of a yoni pod with a throbbing phallus laying in his bed instead of him.

I should check on him, I think while pulling into the University of Washington visitor's lot.

As soon as I park the car, I pull out my phone and text him: **Hey, Matty. I didn't mean to ghost you, I've been camping in Olympic National Park since Friday morning and just got back last night after dealing with an emergency, so I just had too much going on to get back to you. Listen, I'm sorry for whatever is happening to you, but I really don't think what you're going through is something you got from me because I'm fine. IDK if I told you when we met, but I'm a scientist, as are my friends, so maybe I can help you figure it out? I just got back to Seattle if you want to meet up.**

After hitting send, I climb out of the car then walk around to the trunk, grabbing the box containing the small pieces of the pod stalk, the roots, the vein samples, and the pod rind that I aliquoted into small vials of slime from larger samples—because there's no way I'm giving it all to Catie. The only things I didn't bring were the rib bones that I ripped away from the underside of the pod rind flap. The last thing I need is someone other than Julie handling bones from someone who might be a missing person, and I certainly don't need to be associated with another missing person.

As I'm approaching the Genetics-Biotech Center building, the tall, mousy, doe-eyed brunette who I'm here to see appears on the other side of the glass door. "Allie!" Catie says chipperly as she steps outside.

"Hey, Catie," I say flatly, forcing a piss-poor attempt at a smile.

Her big brown eyes look me over. "What's wrong?"

"I'm just worried about Priya and Julie, that's all," I say, handing her the box.

"Don't worry, they'll both be fine, and Julie will be back here at the lab reminding me how messy I am in no time!" She grins.

No, she won't, because she's currently being digested by a freaky pod-thing's sentient asparagus tentacles... It takes everything in me not to cry from the thought.

"Without a doubt," I say, trying to match her expression. "Listen, I got to get back to Hoh Rainforest to see if I can get to Julie before she decides to go looking for us, everything you need to know about the samples and what we need you to test for are in a Word doc on the flash drive in that box. If you have any questions, or if you find out anything, please call me ASAP."

"You got it, Allie!" she says with a nod. "Talk to you soon! Keep me posted on Priya and Julie, okay!"

"Will do!" I say with a wave, wiping away the tears rolling down my cheeks as I turn towards the parking lot.

On the way back to the Honda, my phone chimes in my purse. I sigh when I see that it's Matty and not Priya. *At least I know he's alive...*

Matty: Good to know you're not dead! I've been feeling like I've had the flu since last night, so I was worried that whatever is wrong with me might've landed you in the ICU or the morgue haha. But, yeah, it'd be nice for us to sit down and figure out how this happened. You mind coming here? I'd meet you somewhere public, but I don't have the strength to drive. Been trying to get my ass up and convince myself to go to the ER all morning but I still have a raging boner that won't stop leaking so I'd rather not be in public. That's the other reason I haven't left the house or asked someone to keep my company haha.

Me: Oh shit. That bad, huh? And yeah, I'll meet ya at your place. I still have your address in my Uber history, so just send me your apartment number. Do you need anything? Food? Meds?

He texts me back right after my engine roars to life. **Matty: Can you grab me a few bottles of Gatorade or something? I need something sweet, and I could probably use some electrolytes since I haven't really had anything but water since yesterday.**

He's craving sugar like I was the day after this thing fused to my vagina…

My heart races as I step out of the elevator and walk down the hall to Matty's apartment. *He probably didn't have to text me the apartment number, after all,* I think, staring down at the trail of dried sap that I dripped on the way to his place last Thursday. My gaze then wanders over to the crusty white spots that leaked out of me when I fled his place post-coitus.

Right as I'm about to knock on his door, my hand freezes mid-air an inch away. Everything in me is screaming to leave the Gatorade here, knock, and then run away. But I have to see him so

I can find out how his situation is progressing. I have to figure out a way to help him.

I knock three times, then I wind up standing around waiting for almost two minutes. *Please don't tell me you're dead.* Just as I'm about to knock again, the lock clink-clunks then the door opens slowly.

Matty's exhausted face appears in the gap, his bloodshot eyes at half-mast. If I didn't know any better, I'd say his cheeks look a bit more sunken in since the last time I saw him, not that I was sober enough to remember what he looked like. "Allie," he groans weakly like it's taking everything he's got just to speak. When he opens the door all the way, I see that he's wrapped up in a black blanket. In the corner of my eye, I can see his erection pitching a tent down below.

"Hey, Matty," I say, raising the bag of sports drinks to eye level, doing my best not to stare at his boner. "Got your drinks!"

He flashes me a smile. "Thanks." Now he steps aside and gestures for me to enter. "Smelling as heavenly as I remember."

My lips curl into my mouth and I give him an awkward smile, handing him a bottle as I pass.

"So, you're not sick at all?" he says in a strained voice.

Setting the bag on the counter, I shake my head. "I haven't been sick since winter. What exactly are your symptoms?"

"Fever and chills. Abdominal pain that kind of started around my bladder but now it feels like it's moving up higher, like towards my stomach. And there's this weird, warm, tickling-fizzy feeling in my gut. Almost like hot soda is filling my insides. Uhhhh…"

Oh shit… It's probably the same fizzing I felt when this thing merged with me… If he's feeling it that far up his gut, there's a chance his organs are being liquefied, which means he likely doesn't have long left to live…

"I haven't had an appetite since last night," he continues. "Uh… I got a headache and my head feels cloudy. Oh, and I'm thirsty all the time, and I've been craving sweets like crazy."

"I see… Would you like me to take you to the hospital?"

He shakes his head. "My health insurance doesn't kick in for another thirty days, so I can't exactly pay for a long hospital stay and all the tests and treatments that come along with it. Plus, I'm terrified that they're going to chop off my dick and balls to treat whatever this is, and I'd rather die than let that happen." He lets out a tired laugh. "I'm just going to keep trying this antifungal cream I got from the clinic doc."

"Okay… Are you taking any other medications?"

"Just some Tylenol."

"And has the fever gone down?"

"Barely…"

"Hmm."

"You sure you don't… uh…" His eyes glaze over like his brain suddenly turned off. "You don't have any weird STDs, do you?"

"Nope," I say. "You're the first person I've been with since, like, March. And I've been tested since then. Besides, if I did have an STD, do you really think I'd come back here and face you, or do you think I'd text you about it?"

His head bobbles. "Valid point." Now he starts chugging his drink, gulping obnoxiously loud.

"Besides, I went to my gyno the day before we hooked up and things were all clear, so…" My stomach churns from telling that lie.

He sets down the empty bottle then grabs another from the bag. "So why did cottage cheese only start growing all over my dick after your vice grip of a snatch finally unclamped from around me?" He twists off the top and starts chugging that one too.

I shrug. "How do you know that *cream cheese,* as you call it, isn't something you jizzed into me?"

"*Because* I've beaten off a few times before we hooked up and my jizz has been normal…" he snapped.

I wince. "Well, have you slept with anyone before me? Recently, that is. Because it's possible you caught something from someone and it just took a while to incubate before you came *cottage cheese*. Also, FYI, yeast infections in men can result in chunky, white semen, so it stands to reason that whatever is causing your infection is something similar…"

"I mean, I did bareback some rando a few weeks ago… I guess you could be right about it just taking a while for it to incubate or whatever." He inhales deeply then sighs slowly. "Sorry, I didn't mean to snap or come off like an asshole, I'm just really stressed. I shouldn't have accused you."

I raise a hand in surrender as the guilt from all the lying makes me queasy. "Hey, you have every right to be, so I totally under—"

Suddenly, Matty winces and doubles over, grabbing his erection. "AH!"

"Oh god, are you okay?"

"Yeah, it's just—" He groans during his waddle over to the couch. "Urgh!" he grunts as he flops down onto the cushion. "The moment you walked in, it felt like my dick's started swelling even more—like my body is pumping more blood down there as though it forgot I've had a boner since Friday."

"Oh geez… Have you tried… you know…" I mime whacking-off.

"Uh. Yeah. I tried on Saturday to see if it'd help. But, before I could finish, pus or something started coming out, so I stopped."

"I see…" Hesitantly, I walk over to the couch. "Can I—can I see it…"

"Uh… Are you sure you want to?" he says with a tired smirk. "It's gotten even worse since I sent you those freakshow dick-pics.

Speaking of, I'm sorry for sending those to you. I was in a weird place."

"Don't worry about it. The scientist in me wanted to see those." I force a smile. "And yes, I'm sure I want to see it."

"Remember, I warned you." With a sigh and a groan, he rises from the couch and unwraps the blanket.

Up top, he's wearing a WSU hoody. Down below, he only has on boxers, and his mutated, beige cock is sticking out of the hole in all its erect glory, a glistening glob of amber goo beaded up at the tip. Unlike the pictures he sent me Saturday, his throbbing penis looks almost *exactly* like the spadix of the linga-stage flower that I fucked, just as veiny too. The only difference is, it's not as girthy. His member is still skinny like a carrot the way it was when we had sex.

"You don't look as freaked out as I expected," he says, wincing when his penis pulsates twice in quick succession like a fluttering heart.

"Your dick pics prepared me," I say in awe. "Is it just me or does your dick look longer?"

"Honestly," he mutters, nodding as he stares at it, "I thought it was growing, so I measured it… And yeah, it grew, like, an inch-and-a-half. Guess there's one positive side-effect, huh?" He chuckles nervously.

I force a laugh. "I guess so… Has it spread anymore since the last time you sent me a pic?"

He nods. "*Oh yeah.*"

"May I see?"

"I'm not sure you want to…"

"I do. If you don't mind."

"Why? You turned on by this kind of shit?"

I shake my head. "I just need to see how it's progressing. Things scientists do…"

"Why? Do you have an idea what this is?"

"My best friend has a bachelor's in mycology, so I consulted her and she gave me a list of potential, rare, fungal infections to assess for. If I'm going to help you, I'll need to see everything. So, go ahead and pull those boxers down. I won't freak out or laugh, I promise."

"Fine. Ain't like I haven't sent you a bunch of pictures already." Ever so slowly, he tugs his waistband away before carefully pulling his penis through the hole of the boxers.

"Does it hurt to touch?" I ask.

"No, it's just *extremely* sensitive and fabric really irritates it for some reason," he says, shimmying his underwear down.

That's when I see it—that's when I see the slimy, oatmeal-looking mass that looks *exactly* like the yoni-pod rind spreading outwards from the smooth beige flesh around the base of his cock. Not only has it spread all the way up to just beneath his belly button, but it's grown a few inches down both thighs. At the base of his penis, there are five round, waxy nodules encircling the shaft—what looks to be the beginning of the buds that'll grow into the same petals currently dangling between my legs. Below his cock, the same type of leathery tissue covering his penis looks like it has completely engulfed his testicles.

"It feels like it's spreading back here too," he says, feeling the backside of his scrotum as he turns his ass to me. "Can you tell me if it is?"

Sure enough, the waxy, beige flesh has covered the backside of his scrotum as well. Not only that, but the gooey, tapioca-looking stuff has not only spread up his ass crack, sealing off his butthole but there's a strip of pod rind mass that's grown up to the base of his spine in a perfectly straight line.

I was right… he's turning into a yoni pod and his dick is transforming into a flower-skirted spadix just like the one I found in the tree hollow… This is how skeletal remains got inside the pod we cut open…

Matty turns back around. "Allie?" he whispers.

"Yeah?" I mutter, unable to tear my unblinking eyes away from the sight. "Oh, sorry. Yes, the infection has spread up your butt…"

"You said you wouldn't freak out, but you're staring all wide-eyed at my junk like you're traumatized…" Suddenly, his knees buckle and he plops his bare ass onto the blanket-topped couch.

I blink rapidly, shaking my head to snap myself out of this trance. "Sorry, it's just… I just feel really bad for you, that's all."

"I feel bad for me too…" He lets out a tired laugh. "But I don't think that look on your face is *sympathy*. You look like you've seen a ghost—like you've seen something similar to this before and it terrifies you because you know the prognosis… You've seen this before, haven't you?" He searches my face with those sleepy, half-open eyes of his.

I pause for a long while, taking the time to choose my words carefully. "Now that I'm seeing the way the infection looks on the skin around your penis, yeah. It looks like something I've seen before."

"Well, what is it?"

"I don't know exactly…"

"Is it one of the things your fungus expert friend told you about?"

"Uhh…" I scramble to think up a plausible BS story. "It actually looks like the same weird infection my friend got after our camping trip two weekends ago—after swimming in this pond that had a weird slime mold growing along the shore."

"Was this a guy friend?" he asks.

"No. A girl."

"And did you happen to get intimate with this girl?"

I shake my head. "What? No."

"Then did she use your dildo or something and not tell you?"

"No, because I don't own any dildos."

"Well, did you also swim in the same contaminated water?"

I stare at him all wide-eyed for a moment. "I did, but—"

"So, you *did* give this to me!"

"How could I have if I was asymptomatic?"

"Who knows. Maybe you're the Typhoid Mary of genital slime molds…"

"Again, how do you know your last one-night-stand didn't catch something from swimming in the same pond or catch it from whoever she fucked before you? For all we know, this could be the start of an epidemic, just like that antifungal resistant Candida auris spreading through hospitals."

That gives him pause. "Is your friend's situation as bad as mine?"

"No. She said her infection was, like, a small patch in her crotch."

"One small patch?" he yelps. "Why is mine so bad then?"

I shrug. "Maybe you're immunocompromised?"

"I don't know… I guess that's possible…" He drifts off for a moment. "Did you say her infection *was like* a small patch? Does that mean hers went away?"

I nod, because I want to give him hope even though I know his situation is a death sentence. "Yeah, it did. It was gone in a week."

"Well, shit! How? What medication did she take?"

"Oh, she didn't take any meds. I mean, she did, but the antifungals her doctor gave her didn't work."

"Then what did she do for it? Wait it out?"

I shake my head. "This was my mycologist friend, so, she did some research and whipped up her own batch of ointment ingredients based on natural fungicides and slime mold killing compounds. That could be why me and my other friend didn't show signs of infection. Because she gave us her ointment to use as prophylaxis just in case."

His features relax into a hopeful smile. "Do you—"

"Have any more? I think so. If I do, it's back at my house down in Olympia. If I don't, I can probably get the ingredients and whip some up."

He sighs in relief. "Holy shit. That would be amazing!"

"There's a chance it might not help you because of how aggressive your infection is, so are you *absolutely sure* you don't want me to take you to the hospital?"

"I am *not* going to the hospital, even if this doesn't work."

"Well, do you have someone who can take care of you until you're better? Because you really don't look well."

"Like I said before, I don't want anyone to see me like this," he says, gesturing to his freakish erection as it swells with a slow throb, leaking a slimy, glistening string of goo.

"Then, how about you come with me to my house? I have off this week, so I can take care of you until you're better and monitor you, just in case you get worse."

"Um, you don't mind?"

I shake my head. "If there's even a minuscule chance that this is my fault, playing nurse for you until you're better is the least I can do."

He smiles. "That's really sweet of you, Allie. I don't wanna be alone, so I'll come with ya. Just let me pack a few things."

"I'll help!"

Mission accomplished! Now that I've convinced him to come home with me, all I have to do is keep Matty alive long enough for the doctors to figure out how to treat Priya, then I can get him the medication he needs and stop this shit from spreading!

When he tries pushing himself up from the couch, he flinches and winces. "ARGH! Fucking fuck! Every time I move, it feels like my dick, balls, and bladder are about to explode!"

I stare at the linga-stage mutation between his legs. "You want me to *take care* of you and see if that helps? You know…" I mime jerking off again.

He arches a brow and snickers. "You're kidding, right?"

I shake my head. "Do you have lube?"

His half-open eyes widen, revealing bulging veins strewn across his sclera. "Shit, you *are* serious… You know, you probably shouldn't be touching this…"

"You've been touching it and your hands are fine. Plus, you came in me the day this started and I'm still symptom-free, so I think I'll be okay."

He stares at me in disbelief, blinking rapidly. "There's lube in the top drawer of the nightstand beside my bed…"

"Be right back," I say, walking towards his room. "Go ahead and stretch out across the couch."

"Um… Okay…" All I hear after that is him rustling against the fabric.

I need to find out what happens if he ejaculates during the linga stage of the infection, I think, pulling open his drawer. *That is, if he can orgasm while the linga flower is still mutating his organs…*

By the time I leave the room with his lube in hand, he's stretched across the couch, his eyelids fluttering like he's fighting the urge to pass out.

"Matty?" I say, kneeling on the carpet before him.

"Hm?" he says, peeking at me through squinted eyes. "I'm awake," he says groggily.

"Alrighty." I squirt some lube into my hand. "Just close your eyes and relax. If it starts to hurt or anything, let me know, and I'll stop."

"Okay," he whispers. "I can't believe you're doing this…"

"Me either," I say, curling my lube-coated fingers around his *very* toasty linga.

After two strokes, the leathery erection throbs in my hand, oozing something that looks like a mix between sap and cream of mushroom soup.

Bleh, I think as I stifle a gag. *Maybe this was a bad idea…*

Despite wanting to puke, part of me must be getting super turned on because my petals throb between my legs each time I jerk his rod and there's lubricative sap dripping out of my yoni hole. "How does that feel?" I say in a breathy voice, my chest heaving.

"Honestly? Best hand-job of my life," he groans out.

I keep beating him off nice and slow, giving him a loose-gripped twist every other rise and fall of my hand. When he starts groaning—when his abdomen starts spasming, I know he's getting close to finishing.

"Allie…" My name rolls off his tongue in a strained groan. "AHHH-AH-ARRGH!" he roars, his eyes rolling into the back of his head before his lids squeeze shut.

With that, his cock throbs hard in my hand twice. On the second pulse, a thick, continuous stream of what looks like banana smoothie-colored mucus with red streaks erupts out of his linga-cock like a fucking geyser, sending the powerful jet of gross ejaculate spurting over two feet in the air. Somehow, I manage to scurry back away from the couch right before the goo rope splashes down onto him and the couch. With each subsequent throb, more and more of the filth blasts out of him, each ejaculation firing off with a bit less power and volume than the last. The entire time, Matty's just lying there with his eyes squeezed shut like he's in pain, his core spasming hard with each spurt. At last, after violently spewing out ten squirts from his linga phallus, he finally stops jizzing.

"Holy shit," he says through a sigh, staring in horror at the sludge pooled on his hoody and splattered all over his couch. "Fuck, what a mess… What is this shit? And how did *that* much come out of me…"

"I have no idea…" I say, staring at the scene in awe. "That was legit, like, four cups of cum…"

"Whatever this stuff is," he says, rubbing the goop between his fingers, "it's not *cum*…"

"Yeah… It's probably just discharge," I say as I rise from the floor. "Do you at least feel better?"

"Actually, yeah. I mean, I'm still rock-hard, but at least it doesn't feel like my cock and balls are going to explode anymore…" He flashes me a wince of a smile. "Thanks for that. Sorry it was so gross."

I wave him off. "Don't worry about it." Now I start towards the bathroom. "Just stay where you are, I'll grab some towels so we can get you all cleaned up, then we can head out."

CHAPTER 17
GONE BOY

Tuesday Night, June 7th

After mindlessly pouring the strawberries and blackberries into the pitcher with the banana, I dump in a scoop of protein powder then put the top on. The moment I press the button on this blender to puree the smoothie I'm making for Matty, I drift off into a deep trance. Ever since Saturday, whenever I'm not chatting with or taking care of my one-night-stand turned *patient*, I usually get all spaced out like this. I'm constantly zoning out because I've been perpetually sedated on a steady regiment of blunts and THC edibles to help me cope with everything that's happened since Saturday. Still, even when I'm high, I'm always stressing about something. If I'm not worrying about Priya and how she still hasn't woken up after going into shock, I'm dwelling on how Julie drowned to death in the yoni pod thanks to me.

Currently, I'm not thinking about either of those things. Instead, I'm freaking out about how the guy I'm taking care of is probably a few days away from dying—I'm racking my brain trying to figure out what to do with Matty's body after he fully metamorphosizes into a Yoni pod...

My property line goes a few yards into the woods behind my house. I guess I can dig a hole out there tomorrow near where I buried that egg-seed thing, then I can put the pod in the wheelbarrow and take it out late at night...

That morbid thought isn't something I just began mulling over today, it's something I started thinking about the second Matty said he'd come back with me to my house. There's a reason why, before we left his apartment, I borrowed his iPhone, deleted our text thread, and then stuffed his cellphone in between his couch cushions. Because the last thing I need is cops knowing I was the last person he talked to before disappearing, and I can't have them tracking his phone to my house. Good thing he's been too out of it to even ask about where his phone is…

Eventually, the high-pitched whine of the motor spinning against the low resistance of over-blended smoothie snaps me out of it. Still in a daze, I fill a 1-liter Nalgene bottle with the drink then I stick a bendy straw in it.

"Matty," I say, picking up the plate of mashed potatoes, chicken tenders, and asparagus that I prepared for myself. "It's time to—" My words trail off when I see his monstrous, nude form waddling out through the rear slide door.

I can't help but cringe from seeing how much of his body is now covered in pod-rind. In the two days since he's been here, the chunky, oatmeal-looking mass has spread almost the whole way down to his knees with this connective tissue growing between his thighs that makes it look like his legs are morphing into a mermaid tail. Above that, the mass has covered his entire ass, filling the crevasse that used to be his butt crack.

Oh geez, I think, staring at the pod-rind growth that has spread in a thin, straight line up his spine, stopping just between his shoulder blades now. *It grew that much since I've seen his back yesterday? And why is it only growing up his spine when the stuff on his belly is spreading from rib to rib?*

"Matty?" I call out, setting my plate on the coffee table.

He steps out onto the patio then freezes, groaning as he shields his face from the light of the setting sun shining through the trees.

"Matty!" I say, taking his hand.

As I pull him back towards the door, he turns and looks at me, his jaundiced eyes half-open and unblinking, almost like staring right through me. "Hmm?" he growls deeply, squeezing my hand.

"Come inside. I made you another delicious smoothie for dinner!" I say, shaking the drink in front of his face.

He nods slowly, dragging his feet behind me as I lead him into the house. Now that his thighs have fused together, he has no choice but to walk with a bit of a shuffle like this.

After helping him ease down onto the tarp-covered couch, I slip the straw between his parted lips and tease his tongue until he starts sucking on it.

"Mm! Good, right?" I say with a pitiful smile.

He doesn't respond, he doesn't nod—he just stares blankly at me while sucking hard on the straw.

God, seeing him like this reminds me of how my grandfather was in his final hours. I took care of my pop-pop right here in this very living room those last two days before the liver cancer took him, and it was just like this—he was unresponsive and could only drink instinctually whenever he felt a straw in his mouth.

Matty's only been this far gone since this morning. His mental decline began a few hours after we arrived at my house Sunday afternoon. That night, he was constantly spacing out and kept nodding off mid-conversation. He was so out of it that he didn't even ask me to get him the *homemade ointment* that he came here for. And since I couldn't get him to eat the vegetarian dinner I cooked up, I made him that first super sweet, protein smoothie and he gulped it right down.

Monday morning, he was super out of it and, when I took him out for a walk around the backyard, he started groaning '*Sun. Hurts,*' over and over. Around mid-afternoon yesterday is when he became unresponsive. I had to call him over and over to snap him out of his daze. When he did respond, he kept his sentences short. Then, last night, he started slurring his words.

When I woke up before sunrise this morning, I came downstairs because I heard the wooden floors creaking from him walking around down here. That's when I found him pacing the living room completely naked. That's when I noticed there was this earthy, slightly floral, musty odor to him—the same odor I smelled when I first uncovered the flower's pod. I tried to get him to put his clothes back on, but he just kept shrugging me off and grunting. After that, he pretty much sat around all day today either staring at the TV or staring out the window whenever it got cloudy, paying attention to me only when I fed him smoothies. It wasn't until around sunset that he started pacing and bumping into the rear door, pawing at the glass like a dog who wanted to go out.

"Did you enjoy that yummy smoothie?" I ask, pulling the straw out of his mouth.

His mouth hangs open like he's about to say something but, instead of words coming out, he just drools pureed fruits diluted with saliva all over his chest.

All of the sudden, there's this gurgling, rumble of a noise coming from his stomach. A bubbly, wet burp follows that. The next thing I know, he heaves then projectile vomits a stream of deep pink smoothie swirled with translucent, amber slime all over my chest and lap.

"AHH!" I scream, springing up from the couch and staring at the filth dripping down my cleavage before my gaze wanders to what's dangling from my skirt. "Ewww." It takes everything for me not to throw up.

Without warning, Matty wretches violently again, puking an amber sludge all over his throbbing linga phallus, forming a pool of sludge between his legs that slowly overflows and splatters onto the floor.

*Whatever that is, it looks just like the goo from inside of the yoni pod…
Smells musty like it too…*

"Ah, shit…" I gag. "It's okay, Matty!" I say as I back away from the puddle spreading out from the couch. "I'm not upset, okay? Just stay right there, I'm going to shower quick then I'll come back down and clean you off, okay?"

His unblinking eyes just watch me as I back away.

I'm in such a rush to get downstairs and tend to Matty that I barely dry myself off before scrambling to put on a faded hoody and one of my older skirts.

With an arm full of towels and a bucket full of soapy water in the other hand, I hurry downstairs as fast as I can without falling.

"Alrighty," I say as I step into the living room, "I'm back, Matt—" I freeze in place when I see that, not only is he not on the couch, but that there is a trail of slimy, brown and pink footprints leading to the open sliding door. "Matty!" I call out, dropping the towels and setting the bucket down so hard that it sloshes and splashes all over the floor.

Being careful not to step on the wet footprints, I prance across the room to the back door, clicking on the backyard lights before stepping out onto the foyer.

"Matty!" I scream, scanning the trees surrounding my property.

Unfortunately, my backyard porch lights aren't bright enough to illuminate the woods surrounding my property, so I run back inside, putting on pair of sneakers before grabbing my hiking bag from the garage. Something tells me I'm going to need a compass as well as a flashlight, just in case I lose my bearings out there.

When I get back to the backyard, I find more slimy footprints in the grass leading towards the south, so that's the direction I start walking.

Fucking hell, I need to find him before someone else does, I think, panting heavily as I scan the lawn with my flashlight for footprints and recently disturbed grass.

Upon reaching the tree line, I come across what looks to be a patch of flattened grass and some snapped flower stems—the clues my dad taught me to look for when you're trying to find out if I large animal has recently lumbered through the forest.

The further I venture into the woods, the fewer clues I find. I hike maybe half-a-mile south before doubling back and heading east. After traveling about the same distance, I return to my backyard then head west. No matter which way I go, I don't find any tracks, any linga discharge trails, or any barf puddles.

He's gone... I think as I emerge from the woods and step foot back onto my lawn. *I lost Matty...*

CHAPTER 18
SPOROPHYTE

18 DAYS LATER...
Saturday, June 25th

Alright, I think, finally getting out of bed after laying around all morning. *I need to shower, make breakfast, water my veggie garden—shit, I keep forgetting to water the egg-seed or whatever in the basement. It's been, like, seven days since I watered it last...*

I've been so busy bouncing back and forth between work, the hospital in Tacoma, and my Friday afternoon OB/GYN appointments in Seattle that, by the time I get home every night, I'm usually too burnt out and distracted to remember to go down to the basement and water the spore-ball thing that birthed after my hookup with Matty. Then, on weekends and my off days, I've been leaving at first light and spending most of my daylight hours searching the woods behind my house for my missing *patient,* using a grid search method to eliminate a few squares from my map per day. By the time I get home, my only objective is to eat, shower, and get to Tacoma before visiting hours end. So, before heading out in a bit to pick up Priya from the hospital, I grab the water can from the mudroom then head to the kitchen.

While the container is in the sink filling up, I pull out my phone and resume obsessively googling Seattle and Tacoma local news the way I've done every morning and every evening since Matthew Barlow disappeared from my house, skipping all the stories of the Seattle girl who vanished in Hoh Rainforest almost a month ago. Because I already know they've called off the search and declared her dead. I know that because the park rangers called me a week ago to tell me that after they didn't find her in the BS location that I gave them…

Upon searching Matty's name, I only find the same few articles about him that were posted last week. None of them have been updated and there are no suspects in his disappearance. When I google search and Instagram search **'penis flower,' 'dick flower,'** or **'alien pod'** to see if anyone has stumbled across his fully transformed corpse, nothing comes up, thankfully.

If no one has found it, he's got to be somewhere deep in the woods, which means I have to keep searching, I think, typing **penis mushroom** into Google next. *That'll have to wait until tomorrow. Today is all about celebrating Priya finally being discharged from the hospital.* By the time I look up from my phone, the watering can is overflowing, so I cut off the faucet, dump some water out, then head to the basement.

As the last step groans beneath my foot, my jaw drops from the sight growing out of the cardboard box "Holy shit!" I blurt out.

Rising straight up from the substrate blend is a three-inch-long, white stalk the width of my pinky that leads up into a bulbous, beige growth that's at the bottom of this pale, veiny pitcher plant-like sheath of a receptacle—a sheath wide enough to fit a cock inside of it. The top third of the receptacle is bent at a 90-degree angle, situating it in such a way that the five tiny petals of the flower are parallel to the walls, facing me.

Unlike the linga phallus that I found in that tree hollow a month ago, the petals aren't clamped around the pale stalk like a skirt, they blossomed outwards like a starfish, and the bright red flesh isn't hidden on the underside, it's on full display the way flowers should be. And there's no phallic spadix growing out from between the petals either. In the center of the little flower before me there's a wet, slightly gaped slit that looks remarkably like a vagina. At the top of the slit, it even has a tiny, urethra-like hole under a little clitoris-looking bump too, and both are exactly where they should be in relation to the yoni's tight entrance.

Basically, this true yoni flower looks *just* like the linga flower I fucked but inverted, like someone ripped a linga off the stalk, turned it upside down with the yoni hole and red petals facing front, then attached the spadix's cockhead to the stalk by shoving the white stem into the phallus's *urethra…*

Upon closer inspection, I realize that this little yoni flower's opening doesn't just look like some random vagina, it looks almost *exactly* how mine used to before the linga-yoni merged with me. Like, it even has two thin, parallel flaps of *flesh* encircling the teardrop-shaped gash like labia minora—fleshy curtains that are as long and meaty as mine used to look…

So, Matty's linga kept the shape of his cock after the infection overtook his genitals and my seeds are sprouting into horrific replicas of my pussy? What, is this organism basically a copy-paste fungus or something?

Shining my Galaxy's phone's flashlight on it, I bend the flower upright and spread the yoni flower's soft slit open so I can see straight down into it the hole that leads into the pitcher-like section. Beyond the tight entrance, there's a fleshy, ribbed, wet cavity that traverses the length of the inverted linga shaft before narrowing to a point where the stalk begins.

"Wow, so the yoni flower form of this organism is basically a living fleshlight as opposed to the living dildo I fucked…" I whisper, looking at the shimmering amber liquid pooled at the bottom of the stalk's sheath of a tube.

It's no surprise what would happen if a guy fucked this flower…

I give the flower a sniff. "Damn, this thing smells even more heavenly than the linga flower I fucked!" I sniff it again. "Heavenly and a bit like a real vagina…"

So, when the egg-thingies from my womb burst on a man's penis during coitus, his cock eventually turns to a linga-stage yoni flower then his body morphs into a pod… But if the egg-balls that I birth are planted in soil, they grow into yoni flowers?

The second I poke the flower's slit, the petals flex. And when I slide my pointer finger deep into the yoni seedling's slick tightness, the petals curl inwards ever so slowly only to throb hard as I plunge my digit deep into the soft cavity. "It already feels like a tight little vagina." Not sure why that even surprised me.

When I get done watering the substrate-rich soil, I hurry back upstairs, drop off the watering can in the mudroom, then race across the backyard to the woods to check on the other egg-seed that was planted beside the mutated linga flower testicle.

"Oh my," I gasp when I reach the shady patch of muddy soil where I buried the second egg-seed-spore-ball.

The spot where I place a large stone to mark where I buried the mutated testicle-thing hasn't sprouted anything, as expected. But the spore ball that I birthed has sprouted another yoni flower that's twice as large as the one growing in my basement—about six inches in height with four-inch-long petals as opposed to the one in the basement whose petals are about two inches long.

I just walked by here last Sunday and there wasn't even a sprout… For the flower to be this big already, it must've been developing under the soil and only just sprung up after reaching a certain size or osmotic pressure, much like the parasitic Hydnora Africana plant does… It's only after the flower no longer has me captivated that I survey the area around it and make a discovery. *All the nearby weeds and grass have shriveled up and turned brown… I guess that means the rate at which it grows depends on how many plants are around to parasitize off of… I wonder how big its yoni pod is…*

"Only one way to find out," I say to myself as I start back towards the house.

After grabbing the measuring tape and a shovel from the shed, I venture back into the woods then get to work digging up the soil beneath the dripping yoni flower. It only takes a few scoops for me to uncover the perfectly round pod that's about the size of a cantaloupe—a cantaloupe with thick, kombucha SCOBY for skin. Growing outwards from the front and the back of it are these black, shiny rhizomorph roots, one of which has fused to the root of the nearby tree.

I measure the radius of the gooey-looking pod and get 6-centimeters. "Holy crap, that means this thing is about 37.68-centimeters in circumference!"

A 14-inch circumference is huge for something that I planted a little over two weeks ago, I think giving the pod a gentle poke. Not only is softer and squishier than the massive pod in Hoh Rainforest, but it's hot as fuck like it's full of freshly brewed tea.

Right as I'm finished snapping pictures of the pod and the yoni flower, my phone chimes with a message.

Priya: It's official, I've been cleared for discharge (even though I'm still having discharge)!

Priya again: Sorry, that was a gross joke. Just pretend I didn't send that.

I text her back: **Haha! After everything I've seen since… you know… nothing grosses me out anymore. But, OMG! Yay! I'll be there to pick you up in 35!**

But first, I need to bury this before something comes along and eats it, I think, scooping up a shovelful of dirt and dumping it on the melon-sized pod. *There's no telling what'll happen if a raccoon or something munches on this thing…*

"Holy shit," Priya gasps when she reaches the second to last step of the basement staircase, freezing in place for a moment.

"I know, right?" I reply.

"When you told me the eggs you planted sprouted, I was expecting little linga flowers..." she says, approaching the table.

I laugh. "So was I!"

Hesitantly, she leans in really close to the tiny yonic flower. "It's scary how much this looks like a coochie!" She glances over her shoulder at me. "It looks more like one than—" Her gaze falls to my crotch. "Sorry... I didn't mean to be rude."

I shake my head. "Don't worry about it. FYI, if you were ever curious what my vagina looked like up close before all this," I say, waving a hand over my skirt-covered flower while flexing the petals to bulge against my skirt, "that's almost a perfect replica."

"Seriously?"

"*Seriously.*"

"And you said Matty's linga didn't get all girthy like the original phallus even in the late stage of the infection, right? It just retained its shape and grew a little longer?"

Nodding, I snap my fingers. "Speaking of which, remind me to show you the before and after pictures when we get upstairs. You know, if you want to see them." While I did tell her a bit about what happened with Matty while she was in the hospital, I didn't show her any pictures nor did tell her any graphic details until the car ride home. The last thing she needed while recovering and dealing with PTSD was for me to show her pictures of what could've happened to her had she not been able to fight off the mutagenic infection she got from falling into the yoni pod and getting that pinecone bulb stuck in her vagina.

She winces while nodding. "No, I think I *need* to see Matty's transformation. Because I need to know what worst-case scenario looks like so I can appreciate only walking away with a perpetually slimy vagina that'll forever have fibrous, black roots hanging out of it."

I give her back a rub. "I'm so sorry, Priya..."

"It's not your fault, Allie. Accidents happen. Stop blaming yourself."

"I can't help it… If it weren't for me dragging you and Julie out there—"

"Hey, Julie and I *chose* to go with you because the scientists in us compelled us to see that thing for ourselves." Her jaw trembles as her eyes well with tears. "And if my dumbass didn't fall in the pod, Julie would still be alive, so if there's anyone to blame—"

I wrap my arms around her and hold her tightly. "Let's not do this to ourselves again, okay? Let's just go upstairs, drink some wine, and watch a movie."

She nods against my shoulder. "Okay…" She sniffles. "But first, I need to change my pantiliner. I swear, I'm going to go through ten of these things a day for the rest of my life."

"I guess I know what I'm getting you for your birthday and for Christmas! Every year." I joke, giggling after.

Priya cackles, slapping my tit with one hand while whipping her tears away with the other. "You ass!"

"What?" I say as we head for the stairs. "It's a great idea!"

"You're not wrong. If our research doesn't lead to a cure for my downstairs situation, I'm going to have to ask everyone I know to gift me pantiliners this year before I have to take out a loan to afford them."

"Did the doctors ever figure out if the antifungal meds helped stop the spread of the roots in your leg and vagina?" I ask when we get to the first floor.

She shakes her head as she grabs her purse from the couch. "From the way they made it sound, the lab tests on the root isolates they pulled out of my leg and the slime mass they scooped out of me, the cocktail of drugs *slowed* their growth but, as soon as they stopped plating the drugs on the Petri dishes, the roots kept growing and the flagellated, slime-producing cells kept multiplying."

"So, the drug cocktail basically gave you enough time for your immune system to do its thing?"

"Yup. Well, I mean, the roots in my legs and labia stopped growing, and I fought off the rash after five days, but—" She points down between her legs. "—whatever has colonized in there seems like it's only being kept from growing out of control the way it was those first few days."

"I see…" I say as we stop outside the bathroom door. "Is it bad *down there*?"

She shrugs. "How about you come in the bathroom with me and see for yourself?"

I wince-smile. "For real?"

"Listen, Allie, you pulled a fleshy pinecone out of there, you tugged a rhizomorph vine or whatever out of my uterus, and you fingered globs of chunky goop out of me in the middle of the woods, so I don't really have a reason to be shy about you playing gynecologist with me again." She smirks, opening the door for me and gesturing for me to step inside.

"Hold on, let me get a flashlight."

When I return to the bathroom, Priya is in the middle of pulling down her pants. Like hot cheese being pulled from a slice of pizza, several thick strands of semitransparent mucus are stretching between her vagina and her panties that are now down by her knees. And when she tugs her undies down to her calves, the amber slime strings snap like overstretched gummy worms then swing into her thighs, sticking to them like snot.

"Ugh," she groans, staring down at the jiggling goo pooled in her pantiliner as she steps out of her underwear. "Shit, it's getting on your floor. Sorry about the—"

"Don't worry about it. Better coochie slime than the shit Matty threw up all over me."

"Bleh," Priya gags as she sits on the towel in the middle of the floor. "Okay, doc, I'm ready." With a huff, she lays back and spreads her legs, revealing her glistening vulva and the thick goo oozing out of her tightness like apple jelly from a squeeze bottle.

While the black quills that I couldn't pull out of her labia and her legs have been surgically removed, the black roots are still zigzagged under her flesh like necrotic veins. Unlike how it was after the incident, her vagina isn't all swollen and gaped open, her labia are pressed together in a tight little slit.

"Uh," I hum, shining my flashlight on her cooter. "Do you want me to spread you open or…"

"Oh, right!" She reaches between her legs then plunges the pointer and middle finger of both hands into her tightness. "I'm so used to doctors coming in with a speculum, I forget," she says, pulling her sticky pussy lips apart with a sticky, schlick of a sound. "Fair warning, it smells a little musty sometimes."

Musty, kinda earthy, and a bit floral… Just like the yoni pod smelled when we cut it open…

Beyond the brownish web of slime stretched between her labia, I see them—the horsehair-like fibers protruding from her cervical hole that are floating in and on the layer of slime pooled in her cavity. Well, some of them are just floating around while a few have grown into her vaginal walls.

I'm so captivated by the hairy roots growing out of her womb that it takes a second for me to realize that the inside of her birth canal isn't pink like it once was, it's golden-brown. It's golden-brown because every inch of her vaginal walls and her cervix is glazed with this thick, slightly opaque, gelatinous, amber sheen that resembles a microbial mat composed of milky honey. Also, the entire jelly layer is covered with a web of transparent branched lines, like a slime mold. But that's not all, there are also patches of what looks like yoni pod rind underneath the glaze—one on the right side of her cervix, one where her G-spot should be, and one right underneath where her left pointer finger is stretching open her snatch.

I look up at her, pointing at her vagina. "Do you mind if I—"

"Touch away," she says, looking from me back to the ceiling.

I reach it and poke the glaze on the roof of her vagina just behind her G-spot. My finger sinks right into it as though I've just fingered hot Jell-O. "Oh, it's mushy," I whisper, curling my finger towards the pod-rind nodule with a *come-here* motion, caving a line right through the gelatinous layer like its cake icing.

Priya shivers and her vaginal walls spasm a bit, causing a spurt of brown liquid to bubble out of her cervix. "Oof. What're you doing down there?" A nervous giggle escapes her.

I snicker. "Sorry! I was trying to see if it'd scrape away with enough pressure."

"Oh, yeah. You could rake all that stuff out of me pretty easily with your fingers alone, but it'd just grow back in a few hours. Doctors did it a few times then gave up."

"Oh wow…" I gasp. "Did they end up giving you another hysteroscopy before discharging you today?"

"Yeah, and it's still the same—the inside of my uterus is covered in a web of long, black fibers and there are patches of the pod-rind flesh speckled in the spots uncovered by the roots… But at least it stopped spreading!"

"Geez…" I say, clicking off my flashlight and leaning back.

An obscenely sticky sound emanates below as she pulls her fingers out of her pussy. "Looks like you're not the only one not having kids…"

"Guess we're both going to have to adopt!" I say as I rise from the bathroom floor.

When I offer her a hand, she takes it and gives me this mischievous smirk as I hoist her up. "Since neither of us can safely have sex with a man ever again, maybe we can just get married and adopt some kids together!" Still smiling at me, she turns on the faucet while pumping soap into her other hand.

My cheeks warm up as a grin stretches across my face. "That sounds like a fantastic idea! I mean, we did drunkenly make out freshman year of college, and you *have* fingered my yoni hole—"

"And *you've* been all up in my hoo-ha feeling around twice already!" She giggles, moving over a bit so I can wash my hands beside her.

"*And*, since I'm immune to your situation, we can probably have some *really* hot lesbian sex…"

She snickers. "Scissoring might be fun with those prehensile petals of yours… and I *suppose* we can use a strap-on from time to time."

"Priya baby, you can wear the strap on, but I don't need one. I've gotten pretty good at stiffening my petals, so I'm pretty sure I can slide one right into you."

"Oh wow…"

"Or, if you're feeling *really* kinky, I can close up all five petals like an empty but *firm* banana peel and fill you up *real* good. As sensitive as these things are, that'd feel amazing for both of us." I give her a wink.

"Allie!" Her eyes go wide and her jaw drops as she pulls up her panties. "You freak!" She cracks up.

I lose it. "What? Too far?"

"*Definitely* too far," she says, giving me a little spank on the ass on her way out of the bathroom.

"I don't know, you did look a little intrigued and kind of turned on…"

She avoids eye contact and nibbles on her bottom lip the way she does when she's contemplating something naughty. "No comment…"

"Mm-hm…" I hum, giving her a little nudge. "I mean, I was *kinda* joking, but… if you wanted to… I'm open to it."

When her gaze meets mine, we stare into each other's eyes for a long while. "I mean… I wouldn't say I'm *opposed* to the idea…." A shy smile creeps across her reddening face. "But maybe that's just because your yoni's flower's pheromones have me thinking bad thoughts."

I grin. "I'll bring it up again after we kill a few bottles of wine."

Priya gives me a little wink then we both crack up on our way to the living room.

Right as we start settling down, my phone starts blowing up with text after text.

"Where the hell did I leave my phone?" I ask, checking the table where the wireless charger is.

"Sounds like it's…" Priya says, her words trailing off as she wanders over to where my purse is on the counter. "Here it is! Oh, wow, five texts from Brandon Catalano! And he says…" She squints at the message. "See you next week?" She arches a brow and smiles.

I huff. "That was supposed to be a surprise, Pri… He heard about Julie so he reached out. Then, when I told him you were in the hospital, he booked a flight."

She squeals. "Well, consider me surprised!" She squeals again. "Oh my gawd, I'm so excited! I haven't seen him since graduation! We need to start planning out the weekend! Maybe we should get more of the old crew back together! Wait, is that part of the surprise too?"

I palm the top of her head then ruffle up her hair. "Easy there, brown sugar! You'll find out next week."

CHAPTER 19
WHEN A MAN LOVES A YONI

6 DAYS LATER...
Friday Night, July 1ˢᵗ

"Alright," Priya says, slamming her empty White Claw can on the patio table. "No more drinking for me! I had a long day at work and it's time for bed."

I rise from the sectional the same time she does, staring at Brandon who's on the other side of the firepit from us. "Samesies! Because I don't want to be all hungover and tired tomorrow during our little reunion shindig."

Brandon sighs, slouching in his seat. "Ah, c'mon! I'm still running on East Coast time, so it's like 9:00 P.M. for me! I probably won't be able to sleep for another few hours."

I pat his shoulder as I pass. "There's Hulu, Netflix, Disney+, and Prime Video on the Roku in the living room and in the guest room, so I'm sure you'll find something to keep you busy until you're sleepy!" I say, patting his shoulder as I pass.

He rises from his seat. "You know what? I'm going to grab my laptop and watch a movie out here. I plan on enjoying the outdoors as much as I can before I go back to Manhattan." He winces. "After I *water* your plants."

"Ugh, must you act like a dog every time you drink?" Priya scoffs.

"Pissing outside is just what men do, Pri," he says with a grin.

"Just don't pee all over my vegetables, okay?" I say.

"I'll try not to." He gives me a wink.

"Good night, Brandon!" Priya and I singsong at the same time.

"Night, ladies!"

Halfway through the kitchen, I turn around and walk backward, looking past Priya and watching Brandon disappear into the night. As soon as we turn into the foyer, she mashes those full lips of hers into mine. Playful pecks quickly turn into full-blown making out as I back up towards the stairs. When my heel bumps the bottom step, I pry my face away from hers, take her hand, and pull her behind me up the stairs. The entire way up, we giggle like two school girls.

As soon as we reach the second floor, she wraps her arms around me and we start making out again, exploring each other's mouths with our tongues from the banister all the way to my bedroom. Right as we step into the room, she reaches up under my skirt and delicately fondles my petals, making my abdomen twitch.

"I got you a surprise after work," she says in a breathy voice, slipping a finger into my dripping yoni hole.

"Ah-mm," I moan. Her surprise penetration feels so good, I wind up slamming the door behind me way harder than intended. "Oh, so that's why you were late?"

She pulls her hand out from under my skirt and sticks her sap-covered finger in her mouth. "Mm-hm," she hums, sucking her digit clean. "Strip, get in bed, then close your eyes."

"So, demanding," I say, pulling my dress up over my head on my way to bed.

She stands right in front of the closet watching me crawl back into bed while my petals blossom and close repeatedly. "No peeking!" she says right after I cup my hands over my eyes.

"I'm not!"

All I can hear is some rustling in the closet followed by the sounds of her bare feet clapping urgently against the wood floor towards me. Then the bedsprings groan as she crawls across the mattress.

"Okay, open your eyes!" she says cheerily.

When I remove my hand, I look from her smiling face down to the basket of semi-phallic vegetables resting between us, and my face lights up. There are asparagus, a Japanese eggplant, a skinny corncob, and a long, white radish.

"Priya, this is so sweet!" Giggling uncontrollably, I lean over and peck her on the lips. "Where did you even find a daikon radish?"

Her snicker turns into a naughty giggle. "I stopped at the Asian market to get the eggplants and when I saw that, I was like, '*Allie would love to have this shoved into her flower!*'" She throws her head back as she cackles.

"You know me so well," I whisper, slipping my hand between her thighs and caressing my way up to her hot and insanely damp panties.

She and I make out for a bit, then I help her get her skirt off while she removes her shirt. As soon as she's naked, our mouths meet again. She tickles the fleshy pink underside of my petals while I finger her obscenely slimy gash. Out of nowhere, she pulls her mouth away from mine then kisses me from my neck to my tiny tits to my clit. After licking my sensitive little nub, she lifts my top petal—my most sensitive petal—and sucks on it like it's a flat cock, taking it all the way to the back of her throat. Amazing doesn't even begin to describe how good it feels. If this is what a blowjob feels like to guys, I understand why they love them so much.

About a minute later, she shoves her face in between my flower, plunging her tongue deep into my yoni hole. It feels so fucking good that I can't help but scream and clench around her tongue.

"Shh!" she says, looking up from between my legs, her lips glistening with sap. "Don't forget Brandon's right outside."

"Shit, yeah… Ugh…" I groan in sweet agony when her tongue penetrates my hole again, my petals reflexively clamping around her head like a giant hand.

While she lashes me with her tongue to the verge of climax, all I can hear is her gulping loudly every few seconds, guzzling the sap that I can feel gushing out of me.

I still can't believe this is what our friendship has become, I think, my toes curling as I buck my hips into her face.

What started as a joke last Saturday became reality a day later. Last Sunday night, Priya and I had a few glasses of wine, cuddled up after getting emotional about Julie, then, the next thing I know, she kissed me and her hand slid up my skirt. I asked her if my floral pheromones were making her do that and she just said, *"Yeah, it's making me horny, but it's not making me do anything I don't want to do."* After that, we pretty much hooked up every day since.

When she's done eating out my flower, she sits up, smiling at me with her sap-glazed mouth as she reaches into the basket and pulls out an asparagus. "I washed them all off nice and good while you were in the greenhouse."

"So thoughtful," I whisper, rubbing my clit.

My petals flex into a blossom as she slides the spear tip of the asparagus into my tightness. She toys me with it for a while before swapping it out for the daikon radish. Barely a minute later, a mini orgasm ripples through me. Once the contractions ease up enough for her to pull out the white radish, she stretches me out with the eggplant. Then she finishes me off with the corncob. There are no words for how fucking fantastic those ribbed kernels feel gliding against the ribbed, sensitive flesh of my yoni's tight canal.

It only takes her pumping the corncob in and out of me a few times before I climax so hard that hot, thick sap erupts from my womb, squirting from my yoni hole in quick spurts. Whenever I don't orgasm every other day, this is what happens when the big climax strikes. For whatever reason, my mutated uterus gets engorged with sweet goo and, the more it builds up, the hornier I get. It's only after I climax that the flood gates open and I stop feeling like a nympho in heat. Sometimes spore-balls come out with it, sometimes they don't. Tonight isn't one of those nights.

When I finally come down from the orgasm, I pull her up towards me and we kiss for a bit before I roll her onto her back. It takes a bit of focus because I'm a little tipsy, but I make my flower close up nice and tight, pinching the tips of the petals into the same shape as that daikon radish. Using my hand to hold my clamped, elongated flower like a cock, I tease her slimy slit with the *tip* then plunge it into her hot, gooey pussy.

"AHHH!" she screams as I stretch her wide and fill her deep, transitioning into a quiet moan as my hand covers her mouth.

Having my hypersensitive petals in *banana-mode* pumping in and out of her tightness makes me moan with each thrust. I imagine this is exactly what guys feel when they're balls deep in wet pussy.

Priya's slime-filled cavity gushes with each thrust and squelches every time I retract my petals out of her. It only takes a few minutes of me *fisting* her with my petals pressed together in banana-mode for her to orgasm around my flower. And, when she does, I climax at the same time and collapse on top of her.

"Holy fuck," Priya pants as she strokes my hair. "I love you so much, Allie."

"I love you too, Priya," I say, snuggling up to her and kissing her cheek.

"AHHHH!" a man's voice screams from outside.

Something that sounds like a clay pot shatters right after.

Both of us spring up out of bed, turning to each other with wide eyes.

"Was that—" Priya says.

"Brandon?" I blurt out. "That sounded like it came from the greenhouse…. Oh, god, don't tell me…"

"Oh no…" She grabs her shirt from the other side of the bed and pulls it over her head. "You told him not to go in there… You don't think he…"

I scramble out of bed and grab my dress, my heart pounding. "He's drunk and he's been trying to hide a boner since I picked him up at the airport this morning, so I wouldn't put it past him if he found it… I mean, what guy wouldn't try?"

Me and Priya finish getting dressed about the same time, then we race out of the room. The Monday after Priya got out of the hospital, the six-foot-long, two-foot-high, two-foot-wide cedar planter box that I ordered from Amazon got dropped off by UPS. After she and I put it together, we hauled it in the back of the greenhouse and filled it with soil. The basement yoni flower and its cantaloupe-sized pod as well as the backyard flower and its now pumpkin-sized pod were then repotted into the planter. To keep it protected from light and hidden from anyone who happened to wander into the greenhouse, I planted a bunch of ferns in the trough around it.

I thought that'd be enough to keep any of my friends from finding that genital-looking flower this weekend but, when Priya and I see Brandon on the floor of the greenhouse frantically trying to pull off the hand-sized yoni flower that's clamped around his junk, I realize that I should've gone with my gut instinct and put a lock on that damn door.

"Oh god! Brandon!" I scream, freezing in the doorway.

Brandon looks over his shoulder at us. "Well, this is embarrassing…" he mutters, averting eye contact and looking up to the greenhouse's ceiling while shaking his head. "Yes, this is exactly what it looks like, ladies. I found this fleshlight of a flower, fingered it out of curiosity, and… when I felt how soft and wet it was… well, you can figure out the rest."

"No… No…" I say, staring in horror at the gummy mix of amber sap, off-white cream, and brown sludge that's splattered all over his belly and thighs. The gunk is also all over his fingers and smeared across the palm of his right hand, like he was trying to wipe it off. My eyes wander from the gummy mess to the flower that's tripled in size since I saw it last week. The flower is still attached to the throbbing stem and, from the looks of it, his cock is, like, buried all the way inside of the swollen spathe sheath. The bottom petal is cupped tightly against his balls, and the top two petals are pressed firmly against the flesh between his belly button and penis. With a trembling hand, I reach out to poke the gummy mess on his body only to stop myself an inch away. "Did this stuff—"

"Spew out of the flower's pussy hole?" he finishes. "Yeah. I came in it, and then it *came* all over me." He chuckles nervously. "Then it fucking shot a jet of creamy white shit out of the urethra-looking pinhole—that was right before this tight, fleshy little sleeve swelled around my dick and the petals clamped around my crotch like an angry hand," he says, trying to pull it off of his penis by the stem. Of course, it doesn't move. "God damn, it feels like a starfish is squeezing my crotch! How is this flower so strong?"

That's when I try to peel a petal off of his belly. As expected, it just pulls his skin, which means the flower has fully adhered to him already.

"Ah!" he yelps. "Don't pull it, Allie! They're fucking glued to me or something."

"I was worried that was the case…" I sigh.

"Worried?" he says as his eyes go wide. "Why? What the fuck is this plant, some kind of sexy Venus flytrap-thing? Is that why my dick is getting all warm and fizzy? Because it's digesting my schlong?"

I shake my head. "No, it's *fusing* to your penis…"

"I'm sorry, *what?*" he says, sitting up. "Did you say *fusing?*" At that exact moment, there's a little popping sound, then the stem detaches from the cockhead-shaped growth at the bottom of the beige spathe sheath, leaving a half-an-inch deep hole directly over where his urethra is. Brandon looks down at the scene in confusion as white paste drips out of the thick sleeve still covering his erection like a snug, leather condom. "What the fuck? I was pulling that strong-ass stalk with everything I had since this thing started trying to crush my manhood, and now it just pops off by itself?" He tries pulling the flower off his dick. 'AH-HA-HOWCH!"

"You're not going to be able to remove it, Brandon," I say. "Just leave it before you tear your skin."

"Allie," he says, slowly rising from the floor. "What do you mean I'm not going to be able to remove it?"

"Priya," I say, turning to her. "Do you still have your antifungal ointment and pills?"

She nods, her hand cupped over her mouth, her unblinking eyes staring at our now panicking friend. "Yeah, I left them in the bathroom cabinet just in case we needed to run any experiments," she mumbles.

"Good," I sigh. "Can you grab them, please? If we can treat him early enough, maybe his body can fight off the *infection*."

"Okay, she says, turning and running out of the greenhouse."

"Infection? Hold on, how can I get an infection from a plant?"

"Because, even though it looks like one and smells like one, that's not a plant," I say.

"Then what the hell is it?"

"We don't know exactly, but it behaves more like a fungus than anything…"

"A fungus? *That* colorful, sweet-smelling flower I stuck my dick in is a fungus? What the fuck kind of fungus moves when you touch it and contracts around you when you screw it?"

"The kind with a nervous system…"

"You're kidding me…"

I slip into a trance. "Why, Brandon?" I sniffle. "Why did you come in here? I told you not to go in the greenhouse!"

He huffs. "This might be TMI but, not only has being around you all day had me feeling drunk, but I've been *insanely* horny from the second we hugged at the airport. Been wracking my brain all day trying to figure out why. I mean, you know I think you're gorgeous and that I've always had a thing for you, but this was different. Felt like I was on Viagra any time we were in the same room. And my boner didn't start going down until I went to pee in the bushes after you two went to bed. That is, until I walked by this damn greenhouse and caught a whiff of that same sweet smell you had on you that's been driving me crazy all day. Then, *boom*… I got hard again instantaneously. So I just had to come in here to find out where the smell was coming from and why it was making me horny. Figured you were cultivating an aphrodisiac flower or something. Then… I don't know what came over me… As soon as I moved the ferns and saw it, I felt so compelled to… you know…"

"Fuck, Brandon…" I say, wiping away the tears that just started rolling down my cheeks. "I can't lose you too…"

The look of fear in his eyes at that moment breaks my heart. "Lose me? What the fuck does that mean?! Am I going to die?"

I take him by the hand. "Let's talk in the house, okay?"

His eyes glaze over and he nods slowly like he's in shock.

Just as we're banking right to walk through the patio sliding doors, Priya comes barreling outside with a cup in one hand and a tube of antifungal cream in the other, stopping so abruptly that water sloshes out of the cup and spills all over Brandon's linga-sheathed dick. "Sorry!"

"It's fine," he mutters in a trance, almost staring through her.

"Open your hand," she says. When he does, she extends the tube towards him, but she doesn't give it to him. Instead, she drops two pills into his palm. "Take those then rub this ointment around where the petals are stuck to your skin and anywhere you have yoni gunk on you."

He takes the cup from her. "*Yoni* gunk?" he asks, eyeing me curiously as he pops the pills into his mouth.

"We call it the yoni flower," I mutter, placing a hand on his back and escorting him inside once he's done his water. "The name will make sense once you're all caught up. Now take off your clothes so I can help you apply ointment to the hard-to-reach areas. It's crucial that we don't miss a spot."

Without a word, Brandon strips in the middle of the living room, still in a trancelike state.

When I used to fantasize about him stripping in front of me, this is not what I had in mind...

Once he's done rubbing ointment to all affected areas on his frontside, I takeover and apply some to the edges of the petal clamped around his scrotum like the crotch of a thong before I rub more around the petals glued to each ass cheek. Meanwhile, Priya drapes an old sheet over the couch for him to sit on. And, when she's done, she heads up to my room to grab my laptop.

With the computer on the coffee table before us, I start at the beginning, showing him photos of the linga-stage yoni flower in the tree hollow while I tell him how I came across it. Then I explain what happened when I fucked it. Brandon yelps really fucking loud when I lift my skirt and show him the petals growing out of my vagina. And, when I show him that I can make them blossom and clamp shut, he makes a '*GAH!*' sound and jumps. If wasn't so scared for his wellbeing, I would've laughed at that.

Once he's finished processing that, Priya tells him what happened to her when we went back to investigate the Yoni pod, leaving out details about Julia like we promised we would. After that, I tell him about the eggs-balls that I've been birthing—I tell him about what happened to Matty when we had sex. That's when I show him the slideshow of the progression of Matty's infection, starting with the first dick pic he sent me and ending with the last picture that I took of his pod-rind covered form hours before he disappeared from my care, telling him everything that my one-night-stand went through.

"But…" Brandon says, clicking back through the slideshow. "This happened to this Matty guy because he got the spore-things from the egg on his dick, right?"

"Yeah, but—" I start to say.

"So, you don't know for certain if what happened to him will happen to me since my situation is different, right? Like, I don't have the spores on me, my dick's just stuck inside the flower… So, what if the yoni flower just fuses to me like the linga phallus-thing fused inside of you and it just stops there instead of turning me into a pod monster?"

I glance over at Priya then look back at him. "I mean, I *suppose* that's a possibility, but considering that the flower spewed white cream on you that looks exactly like what was on Matty's dick after he pulled out of me—white stuff that we can't scrape off your skin, it's more likely that things will play out the same way. Except, instead of your penis sprouting petals and turning into the linga spadix like his did, I think you'll skip that step since the flower's sheath and petals are currently fusing to your penis…"

Over and over, Brandon keeps clicking through the slideshow, shaking his head. "So, what you're saying is that the only way to save my life is to get my dick chopped off and have doctors cut away all the skin this goo is plastered onto?"

I don't say anything, I just turn to Priya.

"When I was in the hospital," Priya says, pausing to take a deep breath, "they pumped me full of every single antifungal and antibiotic on the market. They even gave me some experimental stuff. None if it eradicated the roots and slime mass growing *down there*—none of those meds stopped the infection from spawning pond rind patches inside of my womb and vagina…"

"But—but," he stutters. "But you didn't turn to a pod."

"No, it didn't, probably because I'm a woman," she says.

"Brandon," I say. "The working hypothesis is that linga form flower turns women into mobile fruiting bodies while the egg-spores that we produce and the yoni flowers that grow from them transforms men into stationary living dildos that will use its pheromones to enthrall another woman into masturbating in it…"

"The sooner we get you to the hospital," Priya says, "the better chance we'll have to stop this infection from liquifying your organs and spreading through your blood and lymphatic system."

He shakes his head. "No… No thanks! I'd rather die than have my dick chopped off."

"Brandon!" I shout, stomping my foot.

"Allie, my dick feels like is in a condom full of Icy Hot and pop rocks, which means I'm, what, eight or so hours from this thing fully bonding to me?"

I nod.

"And you said that it took that Matty guy four or five days before he started losing his mental capacity, right?"

"I nod again."

He turns to Priya. "And you said that these meds are the only thing that at least slowed down the growth of the roots and slime biomass long enough for your body to fight off the infection, right?"

"Yeah…" she says.

"Alright," Brandon says, nodding, "so then here's what I'm going to do. I'm going to keep taking these pills and using this ointment for two to three days to see if it stops me from turning into a pod-thing. Best case scenario, my dick turns to a linga-whatever and I'll be the male version of you, Allie." He gives me a wink. "Worst case scenario? You bury me in your backyard by the shed and water my dick flower daily to make sure it doesn't wilt…" He grins. "Who knows, maybe then I'll finally get you to make sweet, sweet love to me like you did to the phallus in the woods."

Priya rolls her eyes and scoffs.

I shake my head. "That is *not* funny."

"Hey, gotta crack all the jokes while I can, Allie Hannigan!" he says, nudging me.

"This is a mistake, Brandon," Priya snaps.

He turns to Priya. "You don't know that. Again, my situation is different than that other guy's… If it's not? Well, if things start looking bad by the end of day two, maybe I'll reconsider, okay?"

CHAPTER 20
THE PODLING STAGE

3 DAYS LATER...
Monday

"Allie!" Priya's voice screams from some far-off place beyond the darkness that I've suddenly found myself in. "Allie, get down here!" That command shatters the walls of my dreamless sleep, snatching me from my nap and resurrecting me back to consciousness so hard that I spring out of bed.

"Priya?" I yell groggily, looking from the twilight sky outside my window to the clock only to realize that it's dark outside because it's almost sunset and not sunrise. "Is everything okay?"

"No, It's Brandon!" she screams, her voice sounding strained like she's struggling with something. "You need to get down here!"

The distinct sound of a hand slapping glass follows that.

No, no, no! When my palpitating heart starts pumping adrenaline through me, I go from half-asleep to alert as hell before my feet even touch the floor.

The second I step foot into the living room my eyes widen and well with tears—my legs stop moving and my body goes statuesque as I stare in horror at the sight before me, tears streaming down my face.

Brandon is completely naked, standing so close to the patio door that his face and his fully transformed linga erection is pressed right up against the glass. Just like with Matty, there's a thick strip of pod-rind running up his spine from the mass that's grown over his ass, balls, and thighs. Like something out of a zombie movie, he's moaning and groaning while slapping the glass with one hand and tugging the handle of the locked door with the other. Unlike Matty, he has squishy podling flesh growing all over his hands from the goo he tried wiping off the other night after the flower spewed all over him. Priya, who's just off to the side of him, has one arm wrapped around his torso and she's using all of her strength to try and drive him back to no avail.

How is he this far gone already? We just spoke to each other before I went upstairs to nap...

This horrific, guttural grumble rattles in Brandon's throat.

"Allie, help me get him away from the door!" she yells right as our podling-stage friend pins her against the glass.

Nodding, I rush over and stand on the other side of him. As I snake my arm around his torso, my skin rubs against the squishy pod-flesh that's between his distended abdomen and the part of his pectorals not yet corrupted. With our combined strength, she and I drive him back a few steps. That's when he begins shrugging and thrashing violently. His elbow thumps me in the gut so hard that I stumble back and double over, coughing. Now that I'm out of the way, he grabs Priya by the shoulder and shoves her so hard that she falls and hits the floor with a thud.

"Priya!" I scream, scrambling on all fours over to her.

When I get to her, Podling Brandon hunches forward a bit and lunges towards us like he's about ready to attack. But he doesn't, he just stares at us with crazed and vacant eyes, his mouth agape as brown and slime dribbles down his chin onto his still human-looking chest. My gaze tracks the slime as it streaks down his pectorals to the corrupt pod-flesh covering what used to be his six-pack. As his posture straightens, the petals growing out from the base of his shaft flesh flex into a blossom, beige side of the petals facing us. His petals have been moving like this since they detached from his surrounding flesh last night.

I can't believe how fast the infection spread, I think, watching him cautiously as he turns back to the patio door.

It took Matty about two days to develop a fever and flu-like symptoms, but Brandon woke up feeling like shit ten hours after he got his dick stuck in the yoni flower.

It took almost three days for the egg that burst on Matty's cock to transform his penis into a linga. But for Brandon, the fusion of the flower to his manhood happened overnight. And, just like how I woke up the day after getting the flower stuck in me and could feel everything my yoni felt, Brandon woke up the morning after and felt whatever touched the spadix sheathed around his dick and whatever the petals around the base of his shaft felt.

It took Matty three days to start exhibiting symptoms of cognitive decline and four days before he was slurring his words, but Brandon woke up on that second day super out of it and was having trouble talking before sunset.

Matty didn't strip and start walking around naked in a zombified state until day five, but here Brandon is at that point barely 72 hours into being infected with two times the surface area of his flesh covered in the pod-rind slime mass.

For him to be at this point in barely three days, that must mean there's something about having the yoni flower fused to the penis that speeds up the transformation. Either that or there's something in the gunk the flower spewed on him that catalyzed this rapid transformation.

Now that Brandon is back to tugging at the door handle and banging on the glass, I help Priya up off the floor. "Are you okay?" I whisper.

She groans, looking at me with teary eyes. "Yeah, I'm okay."

I hug her tightly then we stand there watching our friend as he slaps his hand against the door harder and harder, his erect linga smearing streaks of honey-colored discharge all over the glass.

"Allie," Priya says softly. "Remember when we were debating why the pod-rind rapidly grows up the spine while it goes slower across the front side of the body?"

"Mm-hm," I hum, jumping when Brandon pounds the glass with a thunderous strike.

"Remember that YouTube video I made you watch a year or two ago on Ophiocordyceps unilateralis—the fungus that hijacks the brain of ants and makes them leave the hive and cling onto a leaf with their jaw so it can rain spores to other ants?"

I nod slowly. "That could be it… this pod-mass could be rapidly growing up the spine of infected men so it can hijack their central nervous systems…"

"Exactly. And, if that's the case, the yoni flower must be compelling them to migrate somewhere with ideal conditions to complete the metamorphosis."

"Not just compelling them to go somewhere, but compelling them to want to leave near sunset… Because Matty started doing this same thing around this same time of day, and he groaned whenever he stepped into the sunlight…" I say, my words trailing off.

Out of nowhere, Podling Brandon lets out this feral growl then slams his fist into the patio door glass so hard that it shatters a bit, startling us so bad that we yelp and jump. Our harmonious scream makes him glance over at us for a moment before he resumes tugging the door handle.

"What if we let him out?" Priya whispers. "Then we can follow him and find out what happens after a podling disappears into the wilderness…"

"That's actually a good idea," I whisper back. "There's a chance that he might lead us to wherever Matty disappeared to…" I unwrap my arms from around her torso and start walking towards the foyer. "I'll get our shoes."

"Grab rain jackets too. Looks like it's about to rain again."

With our shoes and rain jackets now on, she and I sneak out the front door then walk around to the backyard to grab a shovel from the shed, just in case he drops dead miles from home and we need to dig a hole. Or in case we need a weapon should he develop a taste for flesh like a true zombie.

As soon as Podling Brandon sees us approaching the patio, he tries walking forward as if he forgot there was a barrier between us, cracking his nose and banging his forehead into the glass. That pisses him off so bad that he starts punching the window with more force and speed than before.

"Get behind me, Priya," I say, slipping the key into the lock. Once she's in position, I raise the shovel and turn the key.

As soon as I slide the door open just wide enough for a hand to fit through, his fingers curl around the edge of the doorframe then he uses all his might to slide it open, almost taking my damn hand off in the process. Paying no mind to us, he lumbers briskly by us then waddles his way across the muddy lawn towards the woods to the south.

Three-quarters of the way to the tree line, it starts pouring rain for the second time today. When Podling Brandon feels the precipitation, he looks up to the sky curiously, opens his mouth, and starts flicking his tongue in the air as if he's in desperate need of hydration.

"Poor thing must be thirsty," Priya whispers, holding my hand tighter.

"Was he not drinking the water and smoothies while I was napping?" I ask quietly.

"He was for a while, then he started puking."

"You should've woken me up as soon—" I stop abruptly when Brandon starts smacking his lips loudly, watching him stand there in a daze for a moment before he continues roaming.

Instead of weaving between the gap in the trees, he plows right between the overlapping huckleberry bush and the Pacific Wax Myrtle shrub, groaning as the branches scrape his flesh. Obviously, we go around the shrubbery, slinking between the trees and circling back around to him just as he's emerging through the underbrush.

As he wanders through the woods swerving like a drunk and bumping into trees, he looks around lackadaisically—up and down, left and right—searching for something, or maybe looking around for nothing in particular. Then, maybe fifty yards into the forest, our podling abruptly stops, like he just hit an invisible wall, and he simply stares up at this huge Duncan Cedar tree for a moment. Just as abruptly, he looks down at the mud, drops to his knees, then he starts feverishly digging in the soft soil like a badger.

"I think he's trying to dig a hole to bury himself," I whisper.

"I think so too… Should we… should we help him?" she whispers back.

"I want to, but… maybe we should just observe and record this. Just in case."

"Yeah, okay." She pulls out her phone. "I'll record it if you want to look around here to see if you can find Matty's linga flower sticking up out of a bulge in the soil."

"Good idea," I say.

Walking in concentric circles from where Brandon is digging a hole, I orbit outwards another hundred yards or so. There doesn't seem to be any disturbed soil anywhere around here, and I don't see any phallic flowers sticking out of the ground, so I head back, following the sounds of Brandon's groaning and the noise of hands scooping mud.

When Priya sees me, she mouths: *nothing?*

I simply shake my head.

She and I silently stand in the rain watching Podling Brandon burrow, randomly shoveling dirt in his mouth every so often. As sad as it is to watch one of our best friends dig his own grave, it's incredibly fascinating to see how fast a human who's unencumbered by pain or fatigue can dig a hole with their bare hands.

Somehow, in under an hour, our podling has carved out a six-foot-long, three-foot-deep ditch. Now he's just down there crawling around in a circle on all fours while munching obnoxiously on a mouthful of mud. After randomly stopping to claw at the clump of soil covering the thick Duncan Cedar root for a moment, he suddenly lays flat on his belly and rolls onto his back. He lays there for a few beats before springing up and raking the muddy soil piled at the foot of the ditch back into the hole on top of his legs. Once his legs are covered, he starts scooping the pile of soil to his right down onto his body, burying his abdomen. Then, to cover the rest of his upper half, he claws out chunks from the wall of his ditch until the soil above caves in on him. The last thing we see is him pulling his arms down until the dirt.

"That… That just happened," Priya whimpers, lowering her phone as she stares at the burial plot. "Brandon just fucking buried himself alive…"

"Oh my god…" I mutter, covering my mouth with a hand as tears flood my eyes.

Priya and I turn and embrace each other at the same time. For a long while, we just stand there in the downpour sobbing like that until we can't cry anymore.

CHAPTER 21
THE PHALLUS IN THE BARN SHED

17 DAYS LATER...
Thursday, July 21st

In the backyard of my house right beside the old shed my grandfather built on this property years before I was born stands a new shed—a smaller grey one erected a few days after my yoni-infected friend buried himself. It's a cheap, 8x9 foot barn-style shed with a 6x3-foot rectangular hole cut out of the center of its wooden floor. And rising from near the bottom end of that exposed soil bulge in the middle of that shed is a three-inch-long, white stalk that disappears under a skirt of five petals—petals that are growing down from a veiny, leathery, seven-inch phallus of a spadix. It's the skirted linga flower that's sprouted from the pod below containing the remains of our dearly departed Brandon Catalano.

The day after his podling form buried himself in the woods outside of my house, I pulled myself together and had the shed delivered to my house. Two days later, it was dropped off and some old family friends built it up out back for me that same day. As soon as they left, Priya and I got to work cutting a door-sized hole in the floor. After that, we dug a four-foot-deep pit in the soil with the same dimensions as the hole in the floor. Then, that night, we ventured back to the *burial site* to dig up Brandon's pod. Upon arriving, we were surprised to find that his linga was just beginning to peek through the soil. But that wasn't the only surprise…

After shoveling away the dirt, we didn't uncover Brandon's decaying face and limbs or even a partial human form with slightly more of that slimy mass covering his flesh. Nope, instead, we found a fully formed yoni pod—a pod that had black rhizomorph roots already growing out from the topside where his head was and from the bottom.

Three days of being buried, I think, staring down at my friend's linga growing out of the hole in my shed floor. *That's all it took for his dick to turn into a skinner version of the phallic flower I found in Hoh Rainforest and for his body to metamorphosize into a slightly smaller replica of the pod the girls and I uncovered weeks ago.*

With gloved hands and raincoats on to protect our arms from the rhizomorph roots, we lifted the heavy, jiggly pod out of the ground then gently set it in the wheelbarrow. Once the *grave* in the woods was filled back in, I wheeled Brandon's pod over to the shed then we buried it in there, leaving his erect linga flower above ground, of course.

Every day after work, I sit here in this shed to spend a few hours with my deceased friend before Priya gets home. I sit in here with this buried pod containing my friend's liquified remains, because these pods have a brain and a nervous system and a *body* temperature, so I know he's alive in some fucked-up sort of way.

Sometimes I sit in this lawn chair and read to Brandon's linga flower. Sometimes I talk to him like he's just in a coma or something. Other times I just sit here and fuck around on my phone.

But today, I'm lounging around in here horny as hell from having not climaxed since the night everything went sideways, staring at this beautiful organism's leathery phallus, thinking about what Brandon said to me the night he got his dick stuck in my yoni flower offspring.

"Worst case scenario?" he said to me that night. *"You bury me in your backyard by the shed and water my dick flower… Who knows, maybe then I'll finally get you to make sweet, sweet love to me like you did to the phallus in the woods."*

From that very first weekend we hung out freshman year of college, Brandon had feelings for me. He drunken told me so a couple of times over the years, but I repeatedly broke his heart, friend-zoning him with something along the lines of, *"I like you too, but… I love what we have and I'd never want to do anything to jeopardize our friendship."* He and I did make out once back in junior year of college, but nothing more ever happened between us. Maybe something would've happened that night had I not been dealing with an infection from masturbating with a dirty carrot…

Nothing happened back then and nothing could've happened two weeks ago when you came to visit, thanks to my flower situation. But something can happen now, I think, curling my fingers around the linga and stroking it slowly.

The phallic spadix throbs in my hand, dribbling sap from its tip. It turns me on so bad that my petals blossom in between my legs, making my skirt bulge like three erections just popped up down there. As my heavy leaves throb again, hot honey spurts noisily from my yoni hole. That's when I rise from my seat.

I shouldn't, I think, taking a wide step over the hole in the floor and standing in a bit of a split over Brandon's linga. *But I want to so fucking bad. And if that mutated brain floating in the pod can feel pleasure, I want him to have that…*

Against my better judgment, I squat a bit and curl my fingers around the warm, fungoid-plant *dildo* before lowering myself onto it. "Ah," I whimper as the bulbous head of my friend's metamorphosized cock glides into my obscenely slick yoni hole. I groan in delicious agony as I lower myself further and impale my pussy flower with the phallus, filling myself with it until the linga's petals mash into mine. It's so deep that the glans presses into the sphincter in my corrupt cervix. Up and down, nice and slow, I bounce on the linga, riding it tenderly like I would a male lover.

In a few short minutes, an orgasm explodes down below, and my yoni canal contracts rhythmically around the phallus that has just begun throbbing in me. As I continue riding it a bit slower, sap from my womb gushes down into my canal and spurts out around the leathery rod, making it even more slippery. Unlike the first time I rode a linga, this one isn't swelling in me, and it doesn't feel like it's getting mushy and dissolving whenever I stop to check. It just pulsates faster and faster inside of me like it's ready to erupt.

Maybe it's not swelling and trying to fuse to me because my vagina isn't really a vagina anymore, I think, taking the linga deep one last time.

Just in case I'm wrong, I rise and pull it out of me before the linga climaxes, opting instead to kneel beside it and jackoff the slick phallus. Because I'd rather not have another linga fusing inside my already fucked up vagina situation. A few strokes in, the phallus throbs hard and erupts a thick rope of sap swirled with white paste, spewing it about a foot into the air before it splatters against the soil and the wooden floorboards around it.

"Uh, should I be jealous?" Priya whispers from my left.

My head snaps towards her. "Priya!" I yelp, snatching my slime and gunk-covered hand away from the still pulsating, *orgasming* linga. "You're home early!"

"Yup! It's been a slow week, so I ran out of work to do." She smirks and shakes her head at me, clenching her thighs together. "You just couldn't help yourself, could you?"

"I really couldn't… Even though it doesn't smell that strong to me, I think the pheromones still affect me. And you know how I get now if I don't orgasm in a while."

"Yeah… I know your womb gets all full of sap. I'm sorry I haven't been able to take care of you lately—"

"Priya, don't apologize. It's fine. Neither of us has exactly been in the mood to be intimate since—" I look down at the throbbing, slime dripping linga, "—well, you know. Today was the first day since everything with Brandon that I've felt this way."

She squats beside me and kisses me on the lips. "We'll get through this together." Priya looks from me to the goo on the shed floor. "But this mess isn't something we're going to do together, because I'm not helping you clean *this* up, baby." She laughs as she stands back up.

I giggle. "Don't worry, I wasn't going to ask you to."

"Good!" She gives me a wink. "Here's what I will do for you… I *will* start prepping dinner. And I *will* have a glass of wine waiting for you when you're done cleaning up all this linga jizz."

"Best housemate and best girlfriend ever! Thanks, love!"

"Anything for you, Allie." She walks out of the shed only to pop back in a second later. "Oh, hey. Do you think the linga is going to detach from the stem now that you got it to *cum*?"

My mouth twists to the side. "Hmm… Good question… Not sure that it will since it wasn't doing what the other one did when it was trying to fuse with me. No rapid swelling and the skin of the linga didn't get all mushy and tacky while it was in me."

"Oh…" she says, giving me a look like she's surprised that I fucked the linga before she walked in on me beating it off. "Guess we'll find out in a few minutes then, won't we?"

"The research continues!"

Priya snickers. "Research? Is that what you're calling what happened in here today?"

"Oh, hush!"

"It took me almost twenty minutes to bury the ejaculate-covered soil and scrub the floorboards clean, but I'm happy to report that the linga flower is still attached to the stalk!" I announce as I walk through the patio door. "The thing isn't even limp! I guess that means—"

"Allie, you need to come look at this!" Priya says from the kitchen.

"What is it?" I say, hurrying over to where she's sitting at the island staring all wide-eyed at something on her phone.

"Something you need to see for yourself… You know what, I'm going to stream it to the living room TV."

I follow her to the couch. "Did someone find Matty's linga flower?"

Priya turns to me as she plops down onto the cushion, shaking her head ever so slowly like she's in shock. "Let's just say another phallic organism was discovered… And it's *not* a flower."

"No way," I mutter, sitting so close to her that our arms and thighs are touching.

The YouTube app opens on the TV then buffers for a moment before a video from CNN titled '**Parasite Outbreak: Newly Discovered Uteroboscis Worm Responsible for Increasing Reports of Euphoria & Arousal in Women**' starts up. It opens with this young, beautiful, blonde reporter who's standing in front of a building with palm trees in front of it.

"Trish Childers here, reporting from the beautiful University of Florida campus down in sunny Gainesville, Florida with breaking news that will shed some *much*-needed light on last week's story about the medical mystery affecting women across the nation. Please be advised that this story maybe be inappropriate for younger viewers."

The screen changes to a random montage of women sitting in a doctor's office waiting room only to be replaced by a white screen bordered with red lines that simply reads: **Medical Mystery** at the top.

"Last week, I reported on an uptick of women across the nation who've been reaching out to their doctors about experiencing perpetual arousal, euphoria, and *excessive* wetness." Each of those symptoms appears as bullet points below the **Medical Mystery** title. "After a Florida woman reported several missed menstrual cycles, her gynecologist gave her an ultrasound only to make a startling discovery…"

A screenshot of the black and white ultrasound appears on the screen. In the center of the woman's room is not a fetus, but what appears to be a hotdog-sized worm that's partly coiled up in her organ. From the looks of it, roots are coming out of the thing's head and from its tail—roots that appear to be growing across or possibly into the uterine walls.

"Holy shit!" blurt out.

"Exactly my reaction," Priya whispers.

Trish Childers continues speaking. "After discovering a six-inch worm measuring two-inches in circumference nesting in the woman's uterus, the doctor gave the woman a hysteroscopy and found that the worm's proboscis was feeding on the patient's endometrium while its tail was deeply rooted into the uterine lining, making extraction of the parasite impossible."

Actual footage of the worm inside the milky, slime-coated womb plays while she talks, showcasing the pinkish worm pulsating and squirming as it feeds on the woman.

"After doing a deep dive into research articles in search of any information on womb-feeding parasites," Trish continues, "Dr. Deborah Vincent stumbled across a peer-reviewed paper from last year titled **A Comprehensive Study of the Amazonas Priapus Uteroboscis.** The paper, written by the former Jacksonville University Undergraduate student Lena Anderson who had been studying the parasite since discovering it deep in the Amazonian Rainforest, graphically details the comprehensive research on the behavior, method of transmission, and the symptoms of Uteroboscis infection. As it turns out, Dr. Vincent was able to determine that the perpetual arousal and euphoria her patient was experiencing is being caused by a cocktail of biochemical compounds produced by the worm that drugs the female host, inducing an unsatiable need to procreate. And it is during the act of procreation that the Uteroboscis spreads its eggs to the urethra of the male sexual organ so that he may, in turn, spread larva to another female host."

Now a video starts playing of Uteroboscis worms slithering around in these tanks on top of a lab bench—worms that look *exactly* like veiny penises with slimy flesh the color of raw chicken thighs. And when I say exactly like penises, I mean *exactly*. Their bulbous heads look like the crown of a cock and their smooth, tubular bodies resemble a lubed-up horse penis—they resemble a pink version of a sap-drenched linga phallus. As for the worm's tail end? Well, there's this freaky cluster of red, translucent gummy worm-looking growths sticking out of it—the same growths that were rooted into the woman's uterus in that hysteroscopy video they just showed.

The video transitions back to Trish Childers. "After Dr. Vincent notified the Florida Department of health, local news, and CNN that the reports of the medical mystery popping up across the US were all probably related to an outbreak of Priapus Uteroboscis, our news team learned that Lena has been continuing her research on the womb worms here at the University of Florida where she has been working on obtaining her Ph.D.," she says, gesturing to the building behind her.

"We were told by a graduate student assisting in the research on this invasive parasite that it takes approximately one year for larval worms to reach the size of the one in Dr. Vincent's patient," Trish continues. "Around ten months is approximately when these worms begin secreting the euphoria-causing compounds in their slime. A month or so after that, the eggs not yet implanted in penises during coitus begin hatching inside of female hosts, resulting in what's been seen in the viral videos of girls finding tiny, salmon-colored worms crawling out of their pants."

A montage starts playing. The first clip is of a bunch of girls with blurred-out faces in lacrosse jerseys freaking out in a locker room as worms swarm up their legs. The next one is a go-pro, underwater clip from YouTube of little pink worms racing through the crystal-clear waters of Ginnie Springs towards the girls swimming above the diver. The diver just floats underneath them and watches as the larva disappear into those poor girls' bikini bottoms. The last clip is of another blurred-out girl walking off some water ride in what looks like Universal Studios Orlando. The poor thing is doubled over with both hands on her belly, screaming bloody murder as tons of worms pour out of her shorts with a flood of slime. The women getting off the ride behind her are in a panic, desperately trying to brush the worms off their thighs.

"Since most of the women who've reported symptoms matching Uteroboscis infection are clustered in northern Florida," Trish goes on to say as the video transitions back to her, "this suggests that the outbreak began sometime last summer, likely somewhere near Jacksonville where Lena Anderson lived and conduced her initial research. We are currently in the process of reaching out to Lena to see if the Uteroboscis expert herself can speak on how the outbreak may have happened and if there is any way to remove the worms from the uteruses of the infected hosts. To all the women out there who have been experiencing any of the symptoms mentioned in this report, please reach out to your doctors today and direct them to the article on our website so that they can better help you." As the video cuts to the newsroom, Priya stops the stream.

I turn to her, shaking my head. "Wow…"

"Right?" she says.

"What are the odds that some girl discovers penis-looking, womb-hunting worm in the Amazon Rainforest almost a year before I stumble across a dick growing out of the ground deep in the Hoh Rainforest?" I unlock my phone and google the research article that Lena wrote.

"Slim to none," Priya says through a sigh. "You think they're related? I mean, a worm that makes women horny so they can spread larvae to men and a flower that fuses to women's coochies so she can pop spore-eggs on men's wieners during intercourse has to have some kind of common ancestor, right?"

I shrug. "Anything is possible at this point…"

Priya snickers randomly. "Hey, how much do you wanna bet that Lena girl didn't actually *discover* that phallic worm but that the Uteroboscis or whatever slithered into her while she was exploring, then she just pretended that she brought it back in a jar or something when she took it to her university."

"Oh, there's no doubt in my mind that's what happened if the news is just *now* getting out a year later!" I cackle. "I almost *guarantee* that she's patient zero for the sexually transmitted parasite outbreak. Probably not on purpose, though. She probably had no idea she was passing on larvae or eggs. And, by the time she figured out what was going on, she didn't say anything to anyone because she didn't want to be held responsible for it. Because that's *exactly* what I did with my yoni flower situation, so I know what she probably went through…"

"You're probably right," she mutters, holding my hand. "You think we should maybe go public with what we know before someone stumbles across the linga in Hoh Rainforest or before someone finds Matty's linga flower that's somewhere in the woods near here?"

I sigh heavily. "Honestly, we probably should before more men die from fucking yoni flowers or before some other poor woman has to suffer through what I did…" I stare off into space for a moment. "But if we do that, the cops might for sure tie Matty and Brandon's disappearances to me, making me a suspect in two missing person's cases. Hell, they might pin Julie's disappearance on us too once they find out that we were researching the man-killing fungoid-flower that we discovered in Hoh Rainforest."

"Shit… you're right…"

"All we can do is find Matty's linga flower and take care of it before anyone gets hurt. And we have to make sure no one ever finds out about what's growing in Hoh Rainforest." As those words leave my mouth, my phone chimes with a text message. "Ooh, it's a text from Catie… She says she has a major update for us!" I say, turning to Priya.

"Maybe it's time we bring her into the fold."

I nod. "Probably a good idea since it might help her to know exactly what kind of organism she's trying to sequence. But, if we're going to let her in on what we're studying, we'll need to swear her to secrecy by getting her to sign an NDA or something."

"Good call. Remember my cousin Senna from Boston?"

"The bio major who's working in clinical research, right?"

"Yeah! Well, her dad is a lawyer, so I'll ask him to draft us something about protecting the top-secret organism we're researching."

"Sounds good, Pri! As soon as we get that document from him, I'll invite her over here so she can get up close and personal a linga flower and yoni flower…"

CHAPTER 22
THE MISSING LINGA FLOWER, & OTHER THINGS

Friday, July 22nd

The following afternoon, on my way home from work, I pop into this brick oven pizza place to pick up the food I ordered for us. The liquor store is the next stop so I can buy some more wine and a bottle of tequila, because I'm sure Catie is going to need to get her drink on after she sees what we're about to reveal to her.

Ten minutes after I walk in the house, Priya comes home. About five minutes after that, Catie Holden pulls into the driveway. Since warmed-up pizza is never as good as it is fresh and hot out the box, the three of us catch up over dinner instead of delving straight into science talk. I can barely contain my curiosity during the meal, and the anxiousness makes me eat twice as fast as normal. It takes everything in me not to start drilling her with questions.

"All done?" I say the second that Catie finishes her last slice.

"Mm-hm," she mumbles while still chewing.

"Sweet!" I say, taking her plate and stacking it on top of mine.

"If you can't tell, Allie is really excited to see what you've discovered," Priya says. "Poor thing couldn't sleep all night."

"I could've just emailed you my findings," Catie says with a toothy grin as she reaches down into her backpack. "I wrote up a little report and even made you guys a slide show!" She sets her laptop on the table.

"Aw, that's sweet of you!" I chirp. "But I didn't mind waiting. Thought it'd be nice to treat you to dinner for all your help."

"Well, thanks! I appreciate it!" Catie says, typing her password.

Priya and I set on either side of her, folding our arms on the table so we can hunch closer to the screen. As our resident geneticist clicks through the slides, she explains her findings in great detail. The first thing she tells us is that, whatever this thing is, it has a quadruple helix DNA structure. While it doesn't closely match any known, cataloged plants, fungi, or protists, the yoni samples do share some minor sequence matches with organisms from those kingdoms. For instance, some genes are similar to those that code for fungal cell walls and those that code for rhizomorphs. There are also genes similar to those in plants that code for the enzymes that produce floral fragrances, which is no surprise.

What *is* surprising is that there are sequences that code for mammalian pheromone production, which explains why anyone who smells this thing gets super-horny. She also found fragments of DNA belonging to XX and XY human chromosomes— confirming our suspicions that this yoni plant retains the DNA of the males it turns into pods and the women it turns into fruiting bodies.

"Now," she says, closing out the slideshow and double-clicking on an Excel file, "here is the *big* news I wanted to share…" She zooms out a bit then points to the genetic sequence on the left. "Alright, so this is the genetic code of the orgasm you gave me. The one on the right is—wait, have you all seen the news story about the Uteroboscis parasite?"

"Mm-hm," Priya and I hum harmoniously.

"Just heard about it yesterday," I add.

"Okay, well, being the super-thorough nerd I am, I checked on the NCBI website to see if the researchers uploaded the Uteroboscis's genetic sequence online so I can cross-match your sample against it. Anything that had a codon match between the two organisms, I colored the corresponding cells the same color. As you can see, both the Uteroboscis and the codename *yoni* organism you gave me have more matches with each other than either have with anything else on earth, suggesting—"

"A common ancestor," I mutter.

"Yup!" Catie chirps. "Considering that the worm doesn't have the sequence for yoni cell walls, it's safe to assume there was a genetic divergence at some point, similar to Animalia's split from kingdom Fungi... *But* ...you know how human mitochondria have their own circular DNA that's different from the linear DNA in our nuclei?"

"Mm-hm," we hum.

"And you know how humans have a Mitochondrial Eve that we can trace back to a common female ancestor based on mitochondrial DNA?" Catie continues. "Well, as you know, both the yoni organism and the Uteroboscis have bizarre-looking mitochondria and, as expected, neither one of their circular DNA sequences match any known animal, fungi, or protist mitochondria. *But...*" She pauses and clicks on the other Excel sheet titled **Mitochondria**, bringing up two different sequences that are both mostly highlighted in yellow. "The mitochondrial sequences of both organisms are almost *identical*, which means—"

"Whatever that girl found in the Amazon is more closely related to whatever we found in Hoh Rainforest than anything in their neighboring environments..." I finish, turning to Priya.

Catie nods. "So, can I see whatever this thing is?"

"Of course," I say. "But we're going to need you to sign an *NDA* of sorts. If that's alright."

"Oh, yeah! Whatever, I don't mind."

Once the NDA is signed, I tell her everything—everything except what really happened to Julie and the names of the men who turned to podlings. Priya does, however, inform Catie what happened to her when she fell in the pod. I don't show her any of the pictures or videos though, because I want her to see everything for herself. So, before taking her to the shed, I lift my skirt and show her what the *flower* did to my vagina. Of course, she lets out a shrill scream when she realizes that it's not a prank and that I can make my petals flex into a blossom on command.

Following that, we escort her to the greenhouse so she can see the two yoni flowers hidden in the back—the larger one that was originally planted in the woods and the one from the basement that regenerated a new flower since the Brandon incident. As any curious person would, she sniffs and fingers the pussy-like hole, commenting how it's *"just like a real vagina!"* After that, we take her to the new shed and show her Brandon's linga flower.

"Oh my…" Catie gasps, caressing it from the skirt of petals to the bulbous tip. Her eyes widen when the phallus throbs and oozes a bead of sap from its mutated *urethra.* "I've—I've seen this before, but I didn't think it was real…"

"Huh?" Priya and I hum at the same time, turning to each other briefly before looking back at her.

"What do you mean?" I ask. "When? Where did you see it?!"

"A few days ago. Not in person or anything, it was on TikTok," Catie replies. "That's why I thought it was fake. Here, let me see if I can find it." She pulls out her phone, taps on the app's icon, then she navigates to her favorites. She swipes up over and over and over, eventually reaching videos she liked a week ago. "Shit, I think it got deleted…"

"Of course, it did," I sigh. "It's a video with a dick plant…"

"Do you remember anything about the video?" Priya asks. "Like, was it in the woods? Did it look like it was around here?"

"Uhh…" Catie hums. "It was a video of a girl in the woods filming a skinnier version of this phallus with that TikTok sound that goes, '*At first, I was, like, mmm… feet… as a joke.*' After the '*as a joke*' part of the sound, there was a jump cut to the girl's face as she was doing a naughty, lip-bite thing. She was a super-petite, dirty blonde with gaunt features and blue eyes, maybe about 18-years-old? Anyway, then the sound continued with her lip-synching the '*but, bro… I don't think it's a joke anymore*' part. That's when the video jumps back to the flower's phallus that went from being dry like this to glazed in sap. After that, the camera flips back around to her as she's pulling her hand out of her shorts, then she showed the camera that her hand was covered in that same sap. Behind her, I saw what looked like a red barn with a wooden farm field fence between the woods and the house.

"Oh no…" I gasp, walking out of the shed.

"That explains why the video was taken down," Priya mutters, walking alongside me, looking at me with panic in her eyes.

I stare off in the direction I tracked Matty's slimy footprints too. "There're probably only a few houses with farm fences that border the woods. All we have to do is get on Google maps, find any farms with red buildings that border the woods, then drive to each one." I turn to Catie. "Do you think you'd be able to recognize the house if you saw it?"

She nods. "I more or less have a photographic memory."

"Good," I say, huffing as I start towards the house. "Because we need to track down this linga flower and take care of it before another girl has to go through what I did—before any more guys fall victim to the yoni infection…"

ALLIE & PRIYA'S STORY CONTINUES IN **BOOK 2: *BLIGHT OF THE YONI FLOWER***

Author's Note:

I just wanted to take the time to thank all of you readers out there who have been reading my works on Literotica and sexstories this past year or so. Your comments, emails, and votes keep me going and inspire me to keep writing these deliciously messed up tales.

A special thanks to everyone who has purchased a copy of this book and *The Amazonian Uteroboscis.* Seriously, knowing you all love these stories enough to purchase them with your hard-earned money during these trying times warms my heart! I love and appreciate you all so much that there are no words to describe it. I hope that I can keep showing you how much I love you all by writing more of these tails that you love. And if you'd like to reach out to me on Twitter @BLOverman99 or email (BLOverman99@gmail.com) to chat, feel free to message me! We can talk book stuff, you can send me story suggestions, or if there's a freaky story that doesn't exist and you want it written, please feel free to follow me and private message me and maybe I can write something for ya and post free for you on my publisher's site or Literotica! If you follow me on Twitter, I follow back all of my readers, so I will respond!

For those of you who don't know, authors who write erotica books are unable to promote their books with ads and such, which means that word of mouth and user reviews are the only way to make our works visible on sights like Amazon. So, if you have enjoyed *The Yoni Flower* and *The Amazonian Uteroboscis*, if you could be so kind as to leave a review wherever you purchased this book, that would mean the world to me! Also, if you'd like to keep up with the rest of the series, please head on over to my publisher's website [here at: https://www.scirotic.com/bl-overman] and sign up to the email list. I promise there won't be any spam. There will just be routine updates on my books and similar books to these, messages from me, and treats such as **FREE** epubs/PDFs of samples/short stories/bonus tie-ins that'll be sent out throughout the year.

Thanks again!
With love and appreciation,
B.L. Overman

<u>About the Author:</u>
B.L. Overman

Horror/Sci-Fi Erotica author who writes steamy, graphic, deliciously disturbing tales with unique twists.
Get ready for my next books in the series!

My books so far:

Signup here (https://www.scirotic.com/bl-overman) for release date updates & to get the first few chapters of each book early along with exclusive bonus chapters like Piper's bonus chapters from *Lizzy's Glizzy Flower* (Chapter 22: Throat Cream & Chapter 23: Death By Deepthroat).

Visit my Amazon Author Page to view my catalog:
https://www.amazon.com/author/bl_overman

Follow me @BLOverman99 on Twitter to keep up with updates & come chat with me so we can talk about these books or whatever else you want to chat about!
https://twitter.com/BLOverman99

Or email me if you wanna say hi, talk about ideas, or discuss my books!
BLOverman99@gmail.com